EXODUSTER

BEFORE FREEDOM

A NOVEL

BY KRISTOPHER KING

Ebook ISBN 978-1-7352627-2-7

Print ISBN 978-1-7352627-3-4

__Exoduster:__ A name given to African Americans migrating from the south into new territories post-Civil War.

Table of contents

For CKC

"None are more hopelessly enslaved than those who falsely believe they are free."

Johann Wolfgang von Goethe.

CHAPTER 1

Louisiana 1846
The Boy

He listened to the life slipping away from her; his protector, his teacher, his everything, the matriarch of the Conner clan. Her shallow, raspy breath rattled. His breath was all staccato inhale and sobbing. The suffocating sounds made it uncomfortable for everybody in the room. The Boy felt as any son might, watching his mother leave this world for the next; except he wasn't her son. He was a slave. The dying woman was his owner not his mother. Tears burned and blurred his eyes as he watched her gaze freeze. The feeble, crackling hiss stopped coming from her lips. Her open eyes were dry despite the humid afternoon.

It was a large, opulent bedroom, with a dark oak four-poster bed covered in silk and linen. The floor was rich mahogany with expensive rugs from the farthest corners of the world. Heavy velvet drapes hung aside the leaded glass windows. Sunlight coming through the windows slowed down to match Mrs. Conner's frozen, cloudy eyes. The heavy, damp, mid-summer Louisiana air made it difficult for everyone in the room to breathe.

Ian, in his thirties and the woman's actual son, stood sulking in a corner by the door. Mrs. Conner's lawyer sat in a chair near the foot of the bed and her doctor flanked the bed opposite the Boy. The Boy was one of three slaves kept on the property. He helped maintain the house alongside Lily. Lily stood stoic near the door opposite Ian. Old Tom kept the horses and stable in order. He waited outside with the carriage to take Mrs. Conner to the morgue.

The Boy buried his face in the heavy duvet, trying to forget the room around him. The doctor checked his pocket watch. "I'm declaring time of death at 4:14 in the afternoon," and rose to close the old woman's eyes. The lawyer began to speak, "Well Ian, I suppose we should go over the final will." Not hearing a response, the lawyer turned and looked over his shoulder to where Ian was standing, but the young man had already left the room. The Boy barely noticed that someone was talking, all he knew was that Master Conner was gone.

Both the doctor and the lawyer left the room, ogling Lily as they passed. Her muscles tensed with alarm. She pretended not to notice the stares. She forced her gaze onto the boy, trying to contain the familiar terror that men always sparked deep inside of her. After a moment she exhaled. She reminded the boy that they still had chores to do and company to attend to. "You got five minutes more, boy. Then I need you downstairs."

The Boy's emotional turmoil lulled him into a daydream as he lay next to the dead woman. He struggled with blurry memories of Master Conner. He thought he remembered her teaching him how to tie and shine his tiny shoes. A vague memory of her trying to put a comb through his coarse, curly hair floated up, but he was unsure because Lily mostly did that. His tears and resistance were crystal clear: combing his hair was always painful. He wondered if any of these memories were true, he wanted to ask her. His daydream cracked into focus with the whip and the blood. He shuddered as he remembered that first beating so long ago. It wasn't the clawing scourge whip or the hot blood trickling down his back and legs that frightened him. It was the rage in Master Conner's eyes as she beat him.

He was almost nine years old, sitting on the back porch outside the kitchen. He had abandoned his chores to join Master Ian's two children at play. They were older by a few years but were always kind to him. As they shot marbles together, they chattered about the beautiful swirls of color in the glass balls. Ian Jr. proclaimed that red, yellow, and green made all the other colors in the world. The Boy corrected Ian Jr. "It's blue, not green, and they're called primary colors." Ian Jr. insisted that it was green. The Boy ended the argument by holding up a blue marble and a yellow marble back-to-back in front of the sun. Ian Jr. and his younger sister Samantha squealed with delight at the green hue. Mrs. Conner had overheard most of this exchange from her reading chair. She flew into a rage that ended in the bloody whipping while she screamed that"A nigger never corrects a white, no matter how smart he thinks he is!" *That was right before she got sick,* he thought to himself.

He remembered a lifetime of this type of contradiction. He was taught to read but forbidden to tell anyone. Encouraged to be the best he could be and consistently shown he would never be as good as a white person.

He picked himself up to sit on the bed beside his deceased master. Taking a deep, staccato inhale, he tried to breathe normally. He studied her face; the lines of age like tiny rivers cut into the earth, her paper-thin eyelids so relaxed. He convinced himself that she had his best interests in mind, only wanting to make him a better slave.

Downstairs the lawyer found Ian wondering around outside in the flower garden. The two men stood very close and talked softly at first. The lawyer spoke with urgency and Ian's attention seemed to be on the southern magnolias. The lawyer pleaded with his hands while Ian only shrugged and studied the dirt beneath his shoes. It appeared that the lawyer was losing a fight that Ian had no desire to win.

Lily stood over the sink half watching the two men from the kitchen window and half washing the tea service from upstairs. When Ian and the lawyer left the garden together Lily finished the dishes in earnest. She knew that she must prepare and serve the evening meal soon, even if no one would eat it. Ian's voice startled Lily. The two men were suddenly in the hall next to the kitchen and Ian was yelling that it was his decision now.

The thick mahogany door to the den slammed closed with a great boom, causing Lily to drop a china teacup into the sink. It shattered into a hundred dancing pieces. Terror ripped through her body like lightning. She waited for the inevitable footsteps to come storming into the kitchen. She held her breath until she remembered that Mrs. Conner was gone. She knew the men were too engrossed to care about a teacup. A few more seconds passed as she tried to calm her breathing and slow her racing heart. The now muffled voices of the two men continued unrestrained. Lily began picking up the pieces while trying to make sense of the fragments of overheard conversation.

The Boy floated into the kitchen like a ghost. Lily jumped as she turned from the sink and found him seated at the small wooden table. He did not take his eyes off the tabletop when he asked her what he could do to help. With a heavy sigh Lily let fall the pieces of china into the waste bin like tiny bells. She dusted her hands over the bin and picked at the diamond-like slivers of china that pierced her callused palms. She did not take her eyes from the delicate work as she addressed him. "You wanna help me, you best to help yo' self.

I know you sad about Mrs. Conner. I've been passed around most of my life to these so-called mastas, and she was better than some, but she was still yo' masta, do you undastand me?"

Feeling emboldened by the shouting men down the hall Lily continued. "Those men yellin', they fightin' bout us, you and me, like we part of the house, like we furniture, like dishes they can break and replace without us a say in any of it." She sat at the table and reached out for the Boy's hands. As he pulled away she breathed deep, forced a smile and continued, "Ain't how God intended people to live. I know you undastand me! Please tell me I ain't been wastin' my breath on you all these years. Now leave me be. Go on out to your room and think about what kinda man you gonna be. You ain't no use to me right now anyway." He looked at Lily for the first time. "Yo' time is comin' boy, you gonna be free, out in the world, one way or another. I know it, I know it in my heart."

Upstairs in the old barn the Boy sat on the edge of his single cot made of wood and rope and scanned the room. The roof was gabled, just tall enough for him to stand up straight. One small window let in light. Bare wooden planks creaked underfoot. A change of clothes and his polished shoes lived in the corner. A small vegetable crate stood as a nightstand with a short stack of books next to a candle.

He liked his small room, a space he felt belonged to him. But it was the books that made him happy. They were the world that Lily had spoken of; places and things so far away and so grand that most people he knew would not believe they existed. It was also illegal. He knew he could be whipped or worse for having a book let alone knowing how to read. Lily, or Master Conner—he wasn't sure—had been particularly clear about keeping the fact that he could read a strict secret. He flashed back to a memory of listening to Ian Jr. and Samantha read the newspaper out loud. The Boy smiled to himself. He knew he was getting away with something, like having ice cream before Sunday supper.

He picked up one of the well-worn books. It was an epic tale of brave men in the wilds of the west, his favorite type of story lately. He lay back onto his bed and opened the book. As he stared at the page he wondered if the men in these stories were free. He wondered what freedom meant as the weight of the day pressed down on him. Overwhelmed and emotionally exhausted, he slept.

When he read about exotic places and people he felt unbound, but when he dreamed he would soar. He would travel across time and space to the places that he read about in those books. Today's dream took him to a rugged landscape, like the stories and sketches in the book. A place made of glaciers and granite. A land full of bighorn sheep and grizzly bears, fast, roaring rivers, and slow, sultry sunsets. This land was known as the Montana Territory, and he had been unable to dream of anything else for weeks. The valley he always came to in his dream was as big as the sky. A jigsaw mixture of rolling meadows, full of deer and bison. Sentinel Ponderosa pine trees crowded together to protect mountain lions and their prey. A wide, slow, river wound in and out of armies of trees, cutting the meadow into giant islands of grass and wildflowers.

He pictured himself doing battle with "savages," a terrifying people who lived in caves and ate each other, the way black people lived before being taught about God. He would learn to plow the earth and grow food, hunt meat, wear fur and skins, just like the men in the stories. He believed all this in his dreams, but none of it in real life.

The rolling thunder clapped so hard and loud that he bolted awake. Only to realize it was the large wood and iron doors of the barn beneath him closing. He could hear Thomas, the old stable man, calming the horses and stowing the carriage and tack. The brass and leather making a rhythmic cadence, they mixed with the snorts and hooves of the horses. Above the din of Thomas's work, grunts and groans came shooting up through the floorboards of his room. Some from the horses, most from old Thomas.

He lay still, his eyes fixed on the ceiling, his mind on Thomas. He knew he should get up, but facing Thomas seemed too much to take right now. Thomas wasn't any older than Lily, but a life spent on one's knees, a slave to labor, is devastating to body and spirit. He looked to be a hundred. He expressed himself well for an illiterate man, but he only spoke of sorrow, distrust, and disappointment. Tom's constant babble annoyed him. He wondered how a grown man unable to read could know anything about life. It became overwhelming quickly. He did his best to avoid the old man as much as he could. Sitting on the edge of his bed he gathered the will to face the old man and finish his responsibilities for the day.

Thomas was brushing down the last horse as the Boy slumped down the stairs into the lamp light of the open barn.

"Hey boy," Thomas called out. "You decide to take the day off now that masta done crossed over? You think ain't no one watchin' you boy? Jus' because she gone ain't no excuse to be lazy, besides you makin' Lily pick up yo' chores, and that ain't right and you knows it! Right now be most important to be on yo' best behavior anyways."

The Boy wanted to resist engaging Thomas but fatigue was still pulling hard on him. "I'm going to finish my work now." He headed for the door where he could see the outline of the main house through the darkness.

"Best you understand some things now that she gone," Thomas barked before he could leave the barn. He slouched against a wall of hay with a sigh. Unable to make eye contact while he endured the verbal abuse. He stared at the big man's feet and fought back the stinging tears.

"Times be changin', both out there and in here, and you gone have to learn to deal wit' it like a man. You's a nigga, no matter how pretty you is, and niggas ain't worth the dirt to bury em' with. In fact, you remind them white folks of that every time they see yo' ass, and that there creates what they call resentment. It makes 'em mad that you got they blood in yo'veins, and they gonna treat you even worse fo' it! Now that she gone and her son not wantin' nothin to do wit' you, times gonna get hard fo' you, boy. Mark my words boy, you ain't shit, you ain't never gonna be shit. You best get used to that now and make things a little easier on everybody here."

"Lily says we'll be free one day," the Boy whispered to the floor.

"Some kinda freedom ain't gonna change how white people think of us! These folk ain't never gonna worry 'bout a nigga bein free! Yo'raggedy ass wouldn't know what to do wit yo' self even if you was set free. You jus crawl up in a little ball and shit yo'self cause you ain't shit, I keep tellin' you! Do you even know what bein' free means?" At that the Boy stood and walked into the night towards the main house. Over his shoulder he could hear Thomas convincing himself, or the horses, of all the things he had said.

The house was dark as Lily finished folding laundry in the back room off the kitchen. A single candle burned to light her work. The Boy filled the doorway, startling Lily. "Everything is done," she said. "Just haul the rubbish out to the burn pile and have yo-self in here tomorrow mornin."

The burlap sack was lighter than usual. As he began to heft it over his shoulder he noticed a candle burning in Master

Ian's den. He could see the back of the leather chair, an arm hanging over one side, an empty crystal whiskey decanter on the small table. A bigger-than-life portrait of James Patrick Conner, Ian's grandfather, stared past Ian and into the dark kitchen. The house was so quiet he thought he could hear the old man trying to speak. Like cannon fire, Ian screamed at the portrait of his grandfather. James Patrick Conner was the first of his family to emigrate to the"New World" almost fifty years ago.

CHAPTER 2

Ireland 1789
The Connors

James Patrick O'Conner left the tiny seaside village of Port na Binne Uaine, Ireland in a hurry. He had lived with his parents and his younger brother Joseph in a fine but modest home overlooking a large bay. His father, Cullen O'Conner, worked the local waters as the captain of a fishing vessel. His mother Keelie catered to her family as well as the tight-knit community.

Cullen was the captain of the Faoin Spéir, Gaelic for "Under the Sky." It was a forty-foot Galway hooker, one of the biggest of its day. It brought home enough herring every season to make it one of the most successful fishing vessels in the north of Ireland. As a young boy James had loved the ship. He would often be the first onboard to prepare the vessel for the seasonal trips. He'd race to the docks as she returned, to help empty the hold and scrub down her mahogany decks. He would include the majestic vessel in his evening prayers. He loved watching it from his bedroom window, sitting proud in the marina below. But he could not sail on her.

James suffered from severe seasickness, without fail, on every trip he tried to make with his father. On the last three-day fishing trip James took, he lay crumpled against a bulwark on the aft deck for an entire day. The crew let him be and gently offered encouragement. The captain, his father, was kind and supportive despite his disappointment. Upon their return to port his mother was not so understanding. She put an abrupt end to James's seagoing career and made the boy spend three days in bed. Cullen built the boy up as a man with"solid land legs." A man that would"control industry" instead of breaking his back to produce the supply. Over the years Cullen tried hard to provide James with a firm sense of self.

The family also owned a small farmhouse outside the village of Coleraine. It consisted of a crumbling clay and wattle structure, a small barn, and a garden. Often during the short summer, James would accompany his mother and younger brother to help harvest the tiny vegetable garden.

August was hot. James, his mother, and his little brother were halfway to Coleraine when the horses decided to stop pulling the carriage. James was sore about having to spend the day doing women's work, as the fishermen called it. He was a teenager now and his father's crew liked to tease him. He was also feeling sluggish and irritable from the oppressive heat. He had toiled under the sun before, but today was different. Today the heat not only came down hard from above but also came up from the ground and hung in the air like fire. So when the two gentle draft horses stopped, James seemed to take it personally. He began shouting and jerking hard on the reins, until he noticed his mother and brother staring wide-eyed at him. His already rosy cheeks turned a brighter red and they began to laugh. James laughed so hard that he cried at the same time, the tears and sweat running down his face together. The three laughed wildly. The horses, perhaps caught up in the mirth, began moving again and the family laughed even harder. When they came through the gate of their tiny farm they were still grinning and giggling.

They set about their routine, a little lightheaded from the merriment and the sun. Keelie and Little Joseph gathered the old wooden buckets and hoisted water up from the well. James unhitched the horses so they could get their fill of grass before the trip back. The three of them met behind the barn to determine what was to be gathered.

The small garden was in shambles. Most of the root vegetables were empty holes. All the greens were missing. They stood staring in disbelief. James paced with clenched fists. He kicked at the upturned dirt. He shouted"Who could have done this? I'll make them pay!" Little Joseph began to sob.

Keelie embraced Joseph and with a calm voice said,"Stop being foolish. Someone desperate did this and we should be proud that our hard work fed someone in need." Adding with cheer, "The garden is small, it will take little time to put it right and ready it for next spring."

An hour later they had harvested what remained, raked the rich soil, and loaded the bare crates back onto the carriage. Keelie suggested the boys run down and cool off in the river behind the property while she finished the chores. James and Joseph were off like a shot.

The shaded banks and cold, clear water of the small river was the base of many adventures for the two boys over the years. A canopy of large trees grew along the river. They were a patchwork of greens and browns this time of year, a perfect shelter for adventure. The boys flailed wildly while running downhill through tall grass towards the water. James had a commanding lead over Joseph. He was growing into his strong teenage body. But soon he got ahead of himself and was summersaulting through the wildflowers. Joseph caught up and rolled alongside his brother.

They laughed and hooted until they reached the trees. At the tree line they went quiet. They whispered plans for the sneak attack on the pirates who stole their vegetables. They selected the straightest felled branches for swords and began to sneak into the trees. Joseph was the scout because of his size and stealth. James followed behind, guarding their flanks. They crept along the well-worn paths, listening for the song and clatter of the pirate hoard. They used hand signals to communicate and when they reached the water's edge Joseph gave the signal.

They sprang from shelter and began a furious battle with a half dozen of the world's most dangerous pirates. They fought sword to sword, hand to hand. At once slaying men and assisting each other when needed. The battle lasted a few minutes and Joseph declared the fight a victory. The brothers held their sticks high and cheered. They decided that bringing up the pirate's treasure from the bottom of the river was the next mission. They stripped down to their breeches and dove in.

Even in August the water was cold. The boys came to the surface wide eyed. They tried to make a plan to raise the treasure, but the cold stole their breath. In the intermittent silence they heard faint shouting. The soft but unmistakable sound of men arguing drifted upriver. With a simple glance between them they were shore bound. They dressed with the excitement they had only played at a moment ago. Rushing along the bank, as only children can, swift and stealthy, the voices grew louder. They reached a bend in the small river and knew that the commotion was coming from the other side. They stopped and listened. It sounded like a real fight, and they could not resist the urge to look. James went first, crawling on his belly up onto a mound that the river rolled around. Joseph was right next to him. They were well concealed, and they watched.

Three men in British army uniforms stood in opposition. They surrounded a pot suspended over a fire by a tripod of iron poles. One of the men wore a crisp, clean uniform. The other two looked as if they had been sleeping in the mud for weeks. All three of them were shouting. The boys were entranced. Joseph whispered,"Are those our vegetables?" James signaled his little brother to shut up as he started to notice the surroundings. Strewn about the small fire were the tops of carrots. Tiny bones littered the riverbank. A row of shabby lean-to shelters created a boundary opposite the river. These men had been camped here for some time.

The shouting swirled as the fight escalated. It seemed the dispute was two against one, the well-dressed man on his own and doing most of the yelling. The other two men looked rough, well beyond unkempt. Even to an untrained eye like James's the two men looked dangerous. The boys were feeling more and more uneasy and began to creep down. Before James and his little brother lost sight of the trio, one of the filthy men pulled his pistol and fired a musket ball into the face of his challenger. The explosion was the only sound in the world until the dead thump of the man's body against the muddy bank. Tiny bits of skull rippled the water.

The two men stared at the dead officer. The upper half, the half mutilated by the musket ball lay under the slow-moving river in a cloud of red. The lower half lay heavy in the mud. James was sure that the men would hear his heart beating through his chest. The shriek of a woman pierced the moment.

It was their mother. She had come through the forest behind the row of single lean-tos, and she wore a face of horror as she saw the dead man. The two men seemed as if they had won a contest and the woman was the prize. They were on her before she knew what was happening. James tried to understand how his mother was suddenly a part of this nightmare. Joseph was up and over the embankment and on top of one of the men. This caused an uproar of hilarity between the two men. Little Joseph was restrained with ease. The one holding Joseph said, slobbering, "You can have her. This little one will do."

They began their molestation anew. James felt like he was watching the scene from above as he walked into the camp and picked up a discarded rifle. The man on top of his little brother sat up to undo his trousers. James put the bayonet through his back. The man looked down at the cold steel as James pulled it out hard. He fussed with the hole in his chest, trying to slow the pumping stream of blood while Joseph struggled free. James lifted the butt of the rifle high above the second man's head. He remembered his team winning a cricket tournament a few years ago. The entire town was there. He could see the trophy on the mantel and felt a pang of nostalgia as he brought the rifle down fast with a sickening crack. His mother wriggled out from under the moaning soldier. James, in a trancelike state, wanted the man to stop moving. On the second strike the rifle stock broke and the man was still. The three of them, covered in blood, ran uphill through the tall golden grass to the tiny house. Keelie bloodied her hands bringing up well water to clean Joseph and search for a wound. They hitched the horses and fled in silence.

Cullen was enjoying a pipe on the porch when his fear-some-looking family came roaring into the yard. He did his best to understand the fractured story from his wife as she dragged the two boys into the house. By evening Cullen and Keelie had decided that they would deny being there. They prayed no one would give them up; the locals did not care much for the British soldiers. Heartbroken, they knew that James would leave on the next ship to America.

CHAPTER 3

The Boy

The burn pile smoldered. Not quite a fire but warmer than the surrounding night. The Boy sat down and watched the new rubbish start and stop atop the pile. He could still hear Tom in the distance. He realized why the old man had been so mean; he had just returned from taking Master Conner's body to the funeral parlor. He knew Tom felt as lost and alone as he did. Even more so because he was old.

He watched the smoke float up and away. He thought of Master Conner. He thought of her soul floating up toward heaven and he wondered if she could see him, if she could read his mind right now. He smiled at the thought of her soul as free as the smoke. She had been sick a long time. He felt an unfamiliar joy for her, a kind of lightness akin to the smoke, and in his mind he told her so. Then he thought of himself as smoke, able to rise up and follow the wind to wherever it was blowing. He wondered if that is what freedom feels like, smoke. Someone had once told him that a ship with no rudder was bound to roam aimlessly for eternity. At the time he was concerned for the ship.

He thought of Tom again and felt pity for him. Thinking about the wandering ship now made something inside of him lift a little. He smiled at the thought of the ship, the idea of the smoke, free to wander. But he knew that was not his fate. He knew he could never roam anywhere, he belonged to Master Ian now and that would never change. Lily was the only person that ever tried to argue the point. He knew she was wrong. Memories rose up like smoke.

Mr. Chary was the pharmacist. He was an old Englishman who had recently emigrated to America. After Master Conner fell ill, the Boy was in the drug store often. He became fond of the druggist, marveling at his exotic accent and Mr. Chary's habit of speaking openly with him, something no other white person had ever done. When there were no customers in the store, he would ask the Boy questions and listen to his responses with genuine interest. This made the Boy swoon, sometimes forgetting himself to the point of excitement. They talked about everything from geography to the finer points of hard candy. The Boy always felt a strange urge to express his thoughts and feelings when he was in the store. He didn't understand these feelings, but he liked them. Mr. Chary always asked about"Mrs. Conner," as the world outside the house called her. The Boy described the daily triumphs as well as the failures his master cycled through.

On this particular day he added"God has a plan for Master Conner and that makes everything okay, even her illness." Mr. Chary's eyes smiled and this strengthened the Boy's belief that he was right. Mr. Chary asked,"What's God's plan for you?" This was an example of the delightful way he treated the Boy, and the Boy thought hard on an answer.

The front door burst open with the clamor of the small bell. Two men entered talking about their morning. The noise brought the druggist to attention and he moved quick to attend to the men. The Boy adjusted himself on the tall stool and focused on his shiny shoes as he thought hard on the question. He smiled as Mr. Chary returned.

"What's funny?" the druggist asked.

"God doesn't make a plan for me. He loves me like everything else but it's Master Conner that makes a plan for me. The Bible even says so."

"I don't understand, young man, why wouldn't God have a plan for you when he has a plan for everyone else?"

"God loves everything but he only makes a plan for each man and woman. Us black folk aren't quite that, we still have too much animal in us. Ask anybody. I think you're trying to trick me. That's why I'm smiling."

Mr. Chary paused, his face searching for something. He glanced around the shop and made eye contact with the two men near the front door. They had overheard the conversation and were staring at him with contempt. He told the Boy to run along as he turned and fumbled with the contents on the shelf. The Boy bolted off the stool with enthusiasm. He wanted to rush home and share his new ideas. He stopped short of the two men. He slowed his pace, quieted his footsteps, and turned his eyes to the floor as he passed them.

The afternoon outside the drugstore was held captive by the midday sun. There were no shadows. The town square was empty. The square occupied four city blocks and in the center was a large southern live oak. The grass was bright green and rows of marigolds burst with color despite the heat. There were rows of benches that faced the old tree where people would sit during festivities. Behind the tree were clapboard stands that sold refreshments like roasted peanuts and beer. On Sundays a congregation gathered and the preacher would read the gospel. Most Sundays he and Lily would crowd around the outside of the square with the other black folks and listen. They were not allowed on the grass during the sermon but encouraged to sing along with the hymns. Between where the preacher stood and the tree there was an old stump. It used to be another oak tree. It was two feet by four feet on the surface and three feet high with steps on one side. There was a heavy iron hook in the center of the block. The old stump was worn smooth as stone by the thousands of feet that had stood shackled to the hook. The auctions were on the first Saturday of the month.

The Boy followed his usual route home, crossing directly through the square. When he jumped up onto the old auction block, he thought of the one other occasion the town would gather here to celebrate: when the old tree was used to make an example of slaves who disobeyed the law. These always drew the biggest crowds. He felt a lightness from his conversation with Mr. Chary. Standing on the block, looking up at the tree was proof that he was right.

He remembered that same day as he burst through the door and sped up the stairs to Master Conner's bedroom. He was anxious to share his new insights. He had to pause and gather himself in the doorway. He knew he could not carry his enthusiasm into the room. It would upset the balance of shadows that stayed with Master Conner. Walking as light as he could, he got close enough to the bed that he could see she was awake. His heart leapt as he rushed into a whispered account of his conversation with the druggist. Seeming not to hear him, Master Conner ripped into the bag he'd brought. Lily instinctively entered the room as Master Conner struggled to open the"cough cream." After a sip of the laudanum Master Conner sighed and retreated into sleep.

Lily ushered the Boy out of the room. On the way downstairs he shared his new ideas with Lily. She tried to dispute the idea that she or him, or any person is more or less animal than any other person. She tried to explain that some stories are created to keep people in their place and justify treating them bad. The Boy became defensive. "Tom says you have a false pride because you used to be pretty when you were young."

Lily startled him from his reverie of the past as she sat down beside him at the burn pile. They both smiled at his jolt. They sat in silence and watched the pile smolder. He felt a twinge of regret in his stomach as he recalled the words he had used against her so long ago. He tried to apologize. She didn't understand. He said again all the things he had said to her that day, including what Tom had said about her. Lily felt her skin bristle but said nothing. He expressed his regret once more. She smiled into the heat of the trash pile, the occasional flicker lighting the sadness in her eyes. After a moment she said that she did not remember. He wondered if she was becoming feeble-minded because of her age or if she were pretending not to remember to avoid admitting he was right. Lily loved him like her own and used that love to push away her disappointment in his faulty thinking. "I hope by now you see that I was right," he finally said, wanting her to respond. Her heart broke a little more. The smoke moved to her and added to her discomfort. She sprang to her feet, and with uncommon enthusiasm asked, "How about something sweet from the kitchen?" She turned and ran laughing towards the dark outline of the house. He gave chase.

A single oil lamp cast a glow in the kitchen. Lily and the Boy huddled inside of the light, each with a scoop of honey, warm cornbread, and milk. They talked in whispers and tried hard not to laugh out loud. A dim light shone from under the door of Master Ian's study. They knew not to disturb him. They also knew he would be sleeping off his intoxication and loss.

The Boy told stories of Master Conner and Lily smiled along, humoring him. She focused on his joy, watching his eyes go wide with the fond but mostly made-up memories. Even when he confused Master Conner in place of herself, she would grin and laugh right along with him. Lily delighted in his happiness as a mother would. He was grieving and she would nurture him no matter the cost. Between the laughter, honey, and warm bread they both began talking louder and feeling giddy. Licking the honey from his fingers with a pop, he laughed out loud and shocked them into a sudden silence. They both erupted with laughter. Soft tears filled their eyes as they tried even harder to be quiet. The laughing slowed and they wiped their eyes as the stillness of the house settled over them again.

From the quiet they heard sobbing. Behind the closed door of the den Master Ian was crying. The Boy felt a pang of guilt, he knew that Master Ian had lost his mother. He also knew that Master Ian was always sad ever since his two kids had left for school in New York City. He could only guess at what that might feel like, he did not have a mother or siblings and a strange darkness crept into him. Lily perceived this in an instant. She watched him go to each place and attempt to process the feelings. When he came to that last dark unfamiliar corner she silently panicked. She blurted out, "Your mama was beautiful." She froze, deafened by the sound of her heart trying to break free of her chest. He came out of the corners of his mind and looked into Lily's eyes. He seemed to be searching her face for something. He scanned the kitchen for someone else she may have been speaking to or about. As he looked at her again, she exhaled and waited. A question lingered on his lips but he hesitated. "Do you have a mama?" Not the question she was expecting. She tried to hide her confusion. She took his hand in hers and wanted desperately to embrace him. He smiled at her. Her hands were warm and strong and sticky with honey.

The room erupted with light and noise as the door to the den slammed open. The Boy jumped in his seat and knocked over the glass of milk. Lily froze. The glass hit the floor and shattered. Ian came raging through the kitchen carrying the large portrait of his grandfather. He tore through the screen door, ripping it from the top hinge. He staggered towards the burn pile. He threw the painting onto the pile and watched it light into a small inferno. His body was in full silhouette, swaying with the flame. The burn died. He swung around and zigzagged back up the yard. The Boy and Lily wanted to run and hide but they couldn't move. Ian climbed the stairs and grabbed hold of the wounded door. He jerked it free of the bottom hinge with a splintering screech and tossed it into the yard behind him. He paused, seeing the Boy and Lily for the first time. Without a word he stormed back into his study and slammed the door closed.

Lily and the Boy stared wide-eyed at each other. The room hissed with electricity, shattered glass, spilt milk, and splintered wood. Silence roared from the den. Muscle memory moved Lily to clean up. Something in the yard caught the corner of her eye and she froze. It was Tom, coming from the dark open door of the barn across the long dark yard. The Boy felt Lily freeze and followed her glance to the dark shape of Tom moving through the shadows. Without seeing details of each other's faces, Lily knew Tom was confused and Tom knew Lily was afraid. The three of them knew something was wrong, something beyond the death of Master Conner. Tom stopped in the shadow of the house. Lily began picking up the pieces of broken glass. The Boy wondered why his trousers were wet when a gunshot exploded in the night.

CHAPTER 4

New York City 1789
The Conners

James arrived in the new world sick and afraid. The docks were bustling and indifferent. But James enjoyed a certain insulation, his father had arranged the ship, an apartment, and a job. He had also dropped the"O" from young James's name, not wanting the past to follow him to the new world. Cullen hoped his eldest son would thrive from this elevated start. After two weeks' recovery from the passage, James did just that.

After a six-month trial period as a clerk for the New American Shipping Company, he earned a permanent position. Having an intimate knowledge of ships and their processes, James excelled. He rose quickly through the ranks of the company, spending the entirety of his days at his task. James's personal life did not have the same momentum. After three years he had made few acquaintances and fewer friends.

Meeting Sara seemed to go terribly wrong. His heart had raced, and the words came rushing out, tumbling over themselves. Sara was new to the accounting office, having recently arrived in New York. Her chiseled jawline and sunken eyes still showed the forty-five days of passage from Liverpool, surviving on oatmeal and black tea. The journey was remarkable in that the wind blew so cold it killed three crewmen. The damp wool blanket was her only refuge from the cold and the crowd.

Despite his boyish lack of confidence James could do no wrong in Sara's eyes. They adored each other from the start. Cullen, Keelie, and his little brother Joseph attended the wedding. It was the first time James had seen his family since leaving Ireland. Sara's family was from England. They were too poor to make the round-trip, so James arranged for them to come and stay. The surprise, a week before the wedding, brought Sara to tears. Her everlasting loyalty to her husband-to-be was cemented.

The wedding was lavish. Anyone of any importance was there, celebrities, politicians, businessmen and gangsters alike. Not so much because of James and Sara, but because this fledgling metropolis embraced every opportunity to celebrate.

James and Sara settled into a modest home on Water Street with a view of the river, the ships, and the industry that would make James and Sara wealthy. The New American Shipping Company, or NASCO, owned three ships and leased two more. They traveled a circuit from New York to Liverpool to Le Havre to New Orleans and back to New York. From his home study James could see the masts and topsails in the busy port. On lazy Sunday mornings before church he would marvel at the irony of his world built upon the sea, while he was unable to tolerate it for more than a few moments. After church James and Sara would spend more time at the docks, engaged in the paradox. Sara needed to help the newly arrived immigrants, of which there were a multitude from every corner of the globe.

It wasn't long till Sara was pregnant. Elizabeth Conner was born on a cold winter morning. Fifteen months later another baby girl, Josephine, blessed the Conner family. New York city was exploding with growth and prosperity, as was NASCO and the Conner family too. James was promoted to Chief Logistics Officer and received a seventeen percent stake in the company. Sara agreed, if not whole-heartedly, to stay home with the two girls.

James was on top of the world. His life was full of love and success. He made dreams come true without even dreaming them. Sara was the great inspiration, living her life with a constant sense of duty. She was a strong voice in her church, organizing programs to help feed hungry families. She was also a steady voice for the abolition of slavery. Ships arrived weekly carrying slaves, and Sara did what she could. With the help of her church, she petitioned the port to mandate that a slaver's ship allow volunteers to board with medical supplies. Sometimes she only had water for the chained cargo. James sympathized with his wife; he also did his best to contain her enthusiasm. The restocking and supplying of these ships brought revenue to the port. This made the idea of abolition unattractive although few would speak it out loud. But containing Sara was like trying to put a sweater on a hurricane. He would argue"But that's the way it is," and she would remind him that"God created man!" that"the negroes are men," and that"their lives mattered!"

"An argument beyond reproach for a Christian!" she would finish.

It was usually only Sara delivering these most basic human needs to the slave ships. Occasionally she was accompanied by Dr. Kinder or someone from her congregation. Boarding a slave ship was terror threefold for Sara. On deck she would endure the stares and jeers from a crew that disagreed with what she was doing. Next was the descent into the bowels of the ship. It reminded her of her own six-week passage in the cold, rat-infested hold. These were not the massive Guineamen that carried slaves from the Guinea Coast to the Americas. These were smaller ships that trafficked humans from closer ports in the Caribbean up the coast. Still packed tight, the conditions on board were dire. The last horror was the eyes of the chattel, filled with terror and confusion.

Sara would attempt to make the rounds and at least check that all the cargo was still breathing and provide a sip or two of water. The stench of human waste was overwhelming and the path between shackled bodies so narrow that she seldom made it to all the men, women, and children. Somehow the horror only strengthened her resolve. While exiting the gangway Sara's heart burst with sadness. Until her eyes fell on James and the two girls gathered at the beginning of the pier. Elizabeth waved with a beaming smile. James tickled Josephine as she giggled loud enough for Sara to hear. The gruesomeness she had left behind in the dark was lessened by the light of her family.

Josephine's third birthday was on a cold, clear Sunday. The church service was full of songs sang out in the open spring air. The Conners stopped at the docks on the way home. Sara did her self-appointed duty aboard a ship carrying seven re-captured runaway slaves. Alongside Dr. Kinder, Sara gave water and prayers to the stagnant, silent people chained to the walls and floor of the ship.

They spent the rest of the day in merriment; a party in the back yard, with clowns, cake, and the games children play. The adults enjoyed a great deal of meat on the outdoor stove, and a modest amount of beer. By the evening Sara was dizzy from the excitement. They said goodbye to the guests and cleaned the yard and house of the whirlwind. Sara could see the pure joy in her daughters' eyes as she tucked them into bed. With rosy cheeks the two girls asked if they could have birthday parties every Sunday. Sara promised that Elizabeth's next birthday would be even more grand, and with that they slept with all the happiness of the world.

By Monday afternoon the New American Shipping Company was abuzz with scandal. Late Sunday evening the *SS Opportunity*, a NASCO ship, arrived from Charleston. The Captain reported that as they approached the New York bight, he and his crew witnessed a smaller ship dumping cargo. As they overboard came nearer, the Capitan watched in horror with his spyglass as human bodies were being dropped into the ocean. The twenty-two minutes it took the *Opportunity* to reach the general area proved too much time and not a soul was saved from the black water. The outbound ship was named *Providence*.

James and his fellow executives vowed to follow up on the matter and did their best to calm the shocked staff. On his way home James considered not sharing the news with his wife, wanting to spare her the trauma. He knew it was the very ship she had visited Sunday morning. He also knew that the news would reach her and if it hadn't come from him he would catch hell. He readied himself as he walked through his front door. Dr. Kinder surprised him. Seeing the doctor in his home rang an alarm in James but the doctor's gentle smile disarmed him. Dr. Kinder explained that little Josephine's fever was mild, probably due to all the excitement from the day before. "She was in good spirits, and the fever should break soon," were the doctor's parting words. James and Sara reassured each other and the two little girls. James forgot about the day's events completely, dotting on his family the rest of the evening.

Authorities in Norfolk, Virginia confirmed the detention of the *Providence* and her crew on Thursday afternoon. James decided he would finally be able to share the news. Sara was still sweating out her own fever but Josephine had improved over the last few days. James thought that good or bad, this would take Sara's mind off being sick for a moment. When he arrived home that evening he was surprised to find Dr. Kinder at his house again.

"Twice this week, Doctor, perhaps we should set a place for you at the table." James sensed that this was not a routine visit. With his sleeves rolled and sweat soaking his collar, the doctor sat at the dining room table as James approached.

"Josephine has taken a turn back to fever. Elizabeth came for me an hour ago and we've got her in a cool tub now. I'm afraid it could be yellow fever."

James tore up the stairs and into the bathroom. Sara was in the ice-cold tub with Josephine in her arms. Sara's teeth were chattering as she begged God to help her youngest daughter. Elizabeth stood frozen in the corner as James tried to embrace his wife. She was violent with shivers and didn't seem to notice him. Josephine was red hot and wailing. After an hour James, with the help of the doctor, had the two in bed and as comfortable as they could be. He offered Dr. Kinder a drink.

They sat in the parlor and nursed whiskey that neither of them liked. It was quiet until the doctor spoke." I've studied this new science of phrenology quite a bit. I mean to say that what your wife does for the poor souls on those ships is a grand gesture but—" The doctor paused.

"But what?" James demanded.

"But after all, are these lesser races worth the trouble?"

The doctor had implicated the slave ship into his family's illness and James wanted an explanation. "Blacks have smaller brains and mutated immunities. That could be dangerous for a man or woman of superior genetics," Dr. Kinder offered.

James pressed him for more. "Were those people on the ship sick? Is that why they were throwing them into the bay?"

The doctor, exhausted and unable to confirm any of it slowly put on his coat and promised he'd be back the next day. James did not walk him to the door.

By morning Josephine was dead. Sara, soaked in sweat, lay in bed broken and silent with the girl tucked into her bosom. James sat at the foot of the bed and stared out the window. Elizabeth sat in a corner and wept. Two days later a mixture of yellow fever and heartbreak had taken Sara too. Both James and little Elizabeth were very much alone together.

The NASCO lawyers finally got the official court documents from Viginia. They learned that the crew of the slave ship had fought in self-defense and killed six of the cargo who had escaped their chains. Authorities confirmed that there was no illness aboard the *Providence*. James had not been to work for a week. He listened to the messenger relay the information at his doorstep, but he did not hear any of it. The morning paper at James's feet read"Yellow Fever epidemic ravishes Five Points area of Manhattan!" It went unread by the two remaining Conners.

CHAPTER 5

The Boy

The gunshot was deafening. Lily's hands closed on the broken glass. The Boy jumped, and Tom, in the dark yard, instinctively crouched low to the ground. Everyone knew it was a gunshot but only Tom and Lily had a sense of what had just happened. Tom started for the house as Lily stood and let go the pieces of glass. The Boy moved with purpose toward the den. Lily tried to stop him, pleading, "Wait, please."

Tom came loud through the kitchen door. "Missa Ian!" he shouted, "Missa Ian!" as if he were trying to warn whatever was lurking inside the den. Tom pushed past Lily and the Boy. He paused at the heavy door. He looked back at them. His face filled with dread, frightening the Boy even more.

Tom pushed the door open. It was the large blank space on the wall that they saw first. It had held the oil painting of James Conner. Then it was the smoke lifting from the hair of Master Ian's head. Then the broad back of the winged chair Ian was sitting in. Then back up to the smoke and the hair.

Something was not right with his hair, besides the smoke. Ian's right arm lay out over the arm rest and the old wood and brass blunderbuss was on the floor, also smoking. The Boy knew the noise had come from the gun. He'd heard it at least a dozen times before, but he was confused why master Ian would fire it inside the house. It should be hanging above the small, cold fireplace.

Tom whispered to his master one more time"Missa Ian, you okay?" The Boy started to notice the room. Tom moved into the room and immediately slipped and fell hard to the ground. There was so much blood. The Boy didn't notice it until he watched Tom struggle to get up. The blood was like grease and Tom flailed in it. The Boy remembered trying to catch a bouncing fish on the riverbank. The room was co- vered in blood. It pooled on the mahogany floor, the ornate ceiling dripped with it, there was blood and pieces of bone scattered on the walls. The bone standing out white, pink, and red against the dark wood. The choking sweet smell of rust and gunpowder began to overwhelm the Boy. The thick taste of metal in his throat sent him into the yard retching.

He heaved and gagged on his hands and knees until he noticed Tom and Lily standing over him, arguing. Lily beg- ged,"We should all run. We will end up far worse if we stay." Tom replied,"These folk been good to us fo' a long time, we owe them. Best we stay and take care of things."

"There is nothing left to take care of!" Lily screamed through clenched teeth.

"You got nowhere to go, you can't be out there all alone, Lily. What you think they gonna do to us when they find Ian like that?" Tom stared at her.

The Boy turned onto his back and spoke"He's right. He's right Lily, we've got nowhere to go." Lily resisted the panic. She knelt next to him.

"Baby I know you've had a hard day today, I know you're scared, but this might be the most important few minutes of your life. You gotta be brave. Your masters are gone now and it's time for you to take charge of your own life, but you only have right now to decide."

His eyes locked tight to Lily's. Tom ripped her from the ground and began shaking her and yelling."Woman, you don't know what's good for you! You a uppity bitch! You think you still beautiful!"

The Boy bristled at Tom's anger, but a mix of panic and rage gripped him when he heard Tom crying as he assaulted Lily. Tom hit Lily hard across her face"I love you. I always loved you, and you ain't never seen me!"

He stopped thinking and moved. He stood and looked for something close at hand, something he could use as a wea-pon. He knew old Tom was strong. He flashed on the burn pile, he looked towards the barn, then he saw a shovel on the porch and it was close. Six steps and he had the shovel and was standing behind Tom. Tom had Lily by the throat, lifting her off the ground. Lily was holding onto Tom's hands as tightly as her breath, her eyes were wide and locked on the Boy. Neither he nor Lily could hear Tom cry out, "You never gonna leave me!" as the Boy brought the shovel down hard on the back of Tom's head. Tom collapsed with Lily on top of him. The Boy stood ready to strike again.

Lily wasted no time catching her breath and moved forward. With a raspy voice she instructed, "Go put on extra clothes. Get your boots on and meet me in the kitchen."

The Boy reacted in a daze. He tried to follow her direction, running to his little room and putting on his good leather boots. He sat on his bed and stared at his nightstand with the small stack of books. The blood and smoke came rushing up and he could taste it. He cried. He flashed on what he had done to Tom. As he cried he looked down into his hands. He began to shake. He wanted everything to go back to how it was yesterday. His mind raced. He started to pray but stopped. A feeling of abandonment overwhelmed him. He puzzled on the strange feeling but he remembered Lily, she was waiting in the kitchen. He remembered Tom, he was face down in the yard. The Boy feared that if Tom woke up he might want to kill him. *He tried to kill Lily. Why had Tom been crying? Master Ian hurt himself on purpose.* The room began to spin. He clutched the bed. He forced gasps of breath between sobs and slobber. Choking and breathing, he slowed the panic. He took several deep breaths as tremors ran through his whole body. He wiped his face with the bedspread. He stood and surveyed the room. He wondered how long he would be gone, certain he'd return. He took another deep breath and hurried back to the kitchen, careful not to get too close to Tom lying in the yard. Lily paced the back porch like a caged tiger. The Boy noticed that she wore trousers instead of her dress. With small packs of food tied to their backs, he and Lily stole into the Louisiana night.

CHAPTER 6

France 1792
Lily

Lily was born Lilith Valmont, in France, on the wrong side of a revolution. She was delivered in a bed so big that Countess Valmont's nurse and midwife had to be in the bed with her mother. The elaborate canopy of the bed made the three women look like they were on display in some bizarre carnival tent. The white cotton sheets were so fine that they had a sheen to them and were very slippery, billowing white and blood red. Brilliant light filled every corner of the enormous room. The heavy drapes hung wide open. The window stretched the length of the wall, from the floor to the fifteen-foot plaster ceiling. Outside the window stretched Lily's provenance and fate all at once.

It was a sprawling six square miles of pristine French countryside. Meticulous gardens surrounded the house. Intricate hedges cut into mazes grew further out. On the day of Lily's birth the gardens had almost returned to the wilderness they had been shaped from. The roses, still bright and beautiful, had taken control. The mazes choked on themselves, impossible to pass through. The lavish water fountains had only dead leaves rustling in the dusty porcelain. Of the thirty-five rooms in the sprawling estate only seven were kept heated. Locked doors and canvas furniture covers filled the rest of the estate. Only three of the seventeen staff had remained since the beginning of the revolution. These three were too old for any rebellious blood.

Count Olivier Valmont served the court in Paris. He'd managed to keep his position through the beginning of the revolution by sympathizing with the people and gently criticizing policy.

Olivier thought of himself as a man of the future. He had travelled the world. He fell in love with and married a foreigner. He believed his daughters should have an equal say in their lives. His parents died while he was still at university, so he began making his own decisions early. He was progressive without the sentimentality of the *Declaration of the Rights of Man*. He could see the necessity for reform without forgetting the vital class structure that held his opulent world together.

Most of his peers shunned him, embracing reactionary political attitudes. For four years Olivier Valmont had tried to help forge a new way forward, but France's battle with her enemies and with herself proved too much. Those resistant to change were soon caught up in violence only a desperate populace can produce. The Valmont family fled. Olivier traded his land, title, and most of his wealth for a sixty-acre parcel in the new world. An area named Louisiana, after his own King Louis XIV.

Olivier, Antoinette, and their two children Gwendolyn and Lilith arrived in the port of New Orleans on the hottest day of the summer. The choking humidity was not a stranger to Olivier and his wife; they had met and fell in love in her native Kenya. The two young girls struggled to breathe, knowing only the climate of France. After the five-week ocean passage and the oppressive heat, they were at the limits of civility. But Olivier Valmont had strong and influential connections in the city. They were quickly tucked into the luxury that they had been accustomed to.

Olivier made his rounds around town, meeting old friends, aristocrats who had fled France much earlier. Antoinette did her best to structure the girls' days, piano, ballet, and an English teacher for the entire family. While they were well insulated in the tiny French quarter of the city, they needed income. His friends pointed out the obvious godsend of agriculture paired with slave labor. But Olivier was sympathetic and believed in the premises that, at least in theory, all men deserved basic rights. He believed that outright slavery had no place in a modern society.

The expatriated community had already lost too much. They held fast to what remained of their self-proclaimed supremacy. Olivier decided, with heavy influence, that his sixty acres would be best suited as farmland. He bought one of the last surviving French colonial mansions still standing in the quarter and developed his farm. It produced sugar cane. Less than a year after arriving in the new world Olivier Valmont owned seventy-two slaves.

Managing the new plantation was his top priority and he spent most days away from the city. But Olivier naturally fell back into public service. He spent his evenings engaged with the leaders of his community. They shared ideas and argued the fine points. They drank whiskey and made backroom deals. The atmosphere seemed encouraging, and Olivier began to feel a belonging. He was surrounded by men he thought were of similar thinking.

As the plantation started to make money he looked for ways to move beyond the barbaric methods of slavery and still turn a profit. He hoped to encourage his peers to do the same. His experience during the revolution in France taught him to present unpopular ideas by degrees.

"If we began applying a small portion of each slave's workday towards buying his freedom, we could recoup our investment while encouraging them to work even harder. For surely a free man will out-work an indentured man."

They would nod and agree and even cheer him as he presented ideas to the group. But Olivier soon began to see through the veneer of this society. Instead of challenging an idea outright, members would agree and clap. After the meeting a few men would pull him aside to explain why his ideas were unpractical or unethical. They would argue, "The individual is obligated to sacrifice for the greater good of the whole, independence and freedom is best facilitated through service to the collective of men, not merely to oneself. We all must do our part, and the black savage is conditioned to labor alone."

Olivier would argue that a man can be greater than his condition. His peers would counter that a single man is subordinate. They would insist, "One must dedicate himself to the greater good because everything a man has, he has only because of the collective of men, because of society."

As months passed Olivier found it more and more difficult to deal with the constant duplicity. During public sessions no voice would argue, no man would disagree, but when the vote came down it was almost always unanimous. It became clear that the community labeled themselves freethinkers but remained reactionary. Olivier grew weary; as difficult as France had been during the last few years, it had been at least a good fight. In the new world only trivial matters of money personal to the men in the room resulted in a real argument.

The harder Olivier tried the less the group listened. In frustration Olivier asserted, "No words or ideas are superior to flesh and bone!" They laughed as patience wore thin. They pleaded with Olivier that "to leave a barbarian to his own devices, to let him make his own decisions would destroy the very fabric of this new and near perfect democracy."

The quiet ridicule became more and more conspicuous. An obvious resistance grew against his ideas. The group became so bold as to implicate Olivier's wife and children into the mass of so-called"black barbarians."

"A black ruler of blacks is still but a black herself," yelled one member as he tried to remind Olivier that the economy of the entire region was supported by the labor that moved it forward. They argued that"Slavery is a benefit to the lesser races as well as their own!" and"We are in the new world, and this is how it's done." Olivier's constant rebuttal was that the only thing new about this place was in fact them.

Antoinette was the youngest daughter of a rich Swahili merchant from Malindi and looked every bit the part. She was tall and thin with sharp bone structure and flawless skin. Olivier was also tall and handsome. The young girls were caramel colored with luxurious curly hair. The entire family was beautiful to behold. But Antoinette struggled. She could not understand the barbaric treatment of slaves. Her family had always owned slaves in her native Kenya, but this excessive brutality was new. Growing up her slaves were still people. They had families. The children went to school. They had food and shelter. They lived with dignity. Even though she believed herself superior to the American slave, the dehumanization made her blood run cold. Her discomfort came across as snobbery and further alienated them.

The wives began whispering lies about Antoinette and her children. The community was all too eager to embrace the lies. Overwhelmed in his new life, Olivier reacted with rage when he overheard some of this talk. He made an enemy of the slanderer and found himself committed to a duel. On the morning agreed upon he found himself confused and more than a little frightened. Olivier believed the idea of a duel to be crude, but more to the matter, he had never even held a pistol, let alone fired one. A moment later he was on his back and all his earthly concerns escaped him. He found himself in awe of how quickly the clouds moved across the sky. How pungent the grass smelled. He wondered if his beautiful wife and daughters would forgive him. He was dead before sunrise. His wife and two daughters were arrested with no knowledge of what had happened.

Having no true friends and all ties to France severed, Olivier's wife and daughters were sold into thin air. There remained no proof that the Valmont family had ever existed.

The next morning found the girls in the possession of a broker of human lives. Antoinette had been savagely viola-ted and could not be auctioned until she healed. Within a month all three had garnered top dollar, going to three diffe-rent buyers. Antoinette died before the summer ended. The constant attempt to re-educate her fierce attitude killed her. Gwendolyn, having her mother's strong independence suffe-red a similar fate during the cold winter. Only Lily survived, young enough to adapt to the torture, rape, and brutality.

CHAPTER 7

The Boy

The Boy stared at fingers of the sun poking through the clapboard roof of a strange barn as Lily thought about a plan. He had followed Lily through the night with something like excitement. Down back roads his mind reeled, pushing away the violence of the day. He created small adventures like the stories from his books. But now, tired and hungry, he cried. He cried for master Conner, for master Ian. He believed he cried for his family. A family that he lost in one day. In a hushed whisper Lily tried to talk about plans and routes but he only wanted to return home. Between sobs he said he wanted his room, his books, he wanted his family back. Lily softly told him that none of those things were ever his.

She explained,"Nothing you crying over never belonged to you. We was the property."

His hurt turned to anger and he lashed out at her. "It's your fault! We could have stayed and taken care of master Ian! We could have helped Tom! We had food and a warm house! We were safe!"

This did not come out in a muted whisper but a scream, a wild, uncontrolled, guttural scream. Lily's face blanched as she tried to unfreeze herself and silence the hysterical boy. He was strong, but he relented. It was only a moment before Lily's embrace stifled the wailing back to a sob.

She couldn't remember the quiet and secret place they were hiding in. He didn't understand the danger and Lily knew she could not explain it, again. So she only tried to calm him. Lily breathed to control her own panic. Her heart and mind raced while he was on the verge of hyperventilating. A moment later the adrenaline burned off and yesterday hit them both like the weight of the world. Lily watched the Boy fall into sleep and she struggled to keep her own eyes open. She didn't notice the barn door open until the shotgun poked her in the face.

The woman was tall and gaunt. She was old but had no trouble holding the shotgun. Her eyes bounced back and forth between Lily and the sleeping boy. The moment seemed to drag. The longer it lasted the more Lily expected to see flames erupt from the depths of the two barrels. She wondered if she would see it happen like that or if she would simply die. She flashed on Ian's smoking and disheveled hair.

"You got till dark, then I expect you to clear out," the old lady said without lowering the gun. "I can't believe they call themselves Christians, the way they treat you people." She walked out closing the door behind her. Lily remained still for a few moments, trying to breathe and fight back tears.

The Boy was awake. "Would the lady give us some hot food?"

Lily began to cry. It was the first time in twelve years that she contemplated leaving him to fend for himself. She knew he couldn't grasp the weight of their situation and she feared he would ultimately get them caught. She had decided the moment Ian blew up the night that she would run with the Boy. She would be free or die trying. She knew she had lived free a very long time ago, before she herself could understand what that meant. It broke her heart to even think about abandoning him. She knew that it might be impossible to escape with the Boy.

Determined, she grasped his hands in hers. With quiet rage she begged, "Try and understand what will happen to us if we get caught. They finding Tom right now, blaming him for that bloody mess. They'll hang him before the day is over. It will be worse for us. We can't get caught boy! Do you understand me?"

He had seen hangings, the emptying of bowels, the unnatural stiffness, the gentle swing. The memory frightened him. Her fury startled him. She explained a few of the things done to runaway slaves so that they could still work but never run again. He promised to do as she asked. She encouraged him to rest. In the scratchy hay, under an old, sun leaked roof, they slept.

It was the rats that woke Lily. She knew it was deep into the night. She woke the Boy. They shared some of the biscuits Lily had packed and without a word they left the barn.

Along the dark road Lily lead the way. He would not argue with Lily. He believed she was doing her best for them, but he also believed she did not truly understand what was best. He knew they should have stayed and carried on the Conner's estate, and that whoever took over would have taken care of them. The Boy did not understand what they were trying to escape.

Lily often spoke of freedom. The Boy wondered what part of Lily wasn't free. He knew it was a common concept. He read about it in books, but he could never put a finger on the true meaning of the word freedom. In his eyes Lily was free, free to think for herself, free to carry out her daily responsibilities. What was it she wanted to do that she could not? He didn't understand. Running away didn't feel like freedom.

They walked the footpath between farms and along streams. They passed livestock and lightless farmhouses. He was sure that he was free. He told himself that it was up to him to take the coffee tray up to master Conner, or how to grind the coffee in the first place. It was up to him to help Tom with the horses or not; Tom was a capable man. He decided what to wear or when to shine his shoes. It seemed to him that he was in control of his life, as was Lily. They had as much freedom as a black could wish for. He knew that Lily, as much as he loved her, was wrong. She might be too proud or, as the Bible warns, caught in a self-possessed pride. For years Tom would whisper these things about Lily and now he believed old Tom was right all along. He wondered what Tom was doing. He felt bad about hitting him and hoped he was not too mad. He thought about what Lily had said and knew nobody could blame old Tom for master Ian's accident.

Maryland 1822
Tom

Tom smiled while he worked, even as a young boy. He smiled in the fields while pulling cotton from the bush. He smiled in the barn while brushing down the large draft animals. Even when his owners strapped him in the heavy leather harness and made him pull the plow for their own amusement, Tom would smile, happy to please somebody.

Tom was born strong. After a year of nursing, he was taken from his mother. She did not cry. She had lived through this seven times, but baby Tom knew no better and screamed at the separation. It would be the only time in his life he would cry out loud.

Being big and muscular he found purpose in manual labor. He understood that hard work pleased his master and the overseer. He worked harder knowing this. He enjoyed the benefits of being liked by his owners. He struggled to understand some of the other folks' resentment. He believed his owner who told him to do his work and never talk back so he would find reward in the kingdom of God. He believed the preacher, who on Sundays would preach the same thing. He also believed the dogs and men that would bring back a slave who had run in the night. He believed the violence that would fall upon the runner, the blood and bones lost. He believed in this way of life. He knew that if he did as he was told and looked after his master that he would be treated fair.

Somewhere near his thirty-fifth year Tom and his wife sat on the porch watching the sun dip into the Maryland horizon. They waited for the twins, Elbert and Enos, to return from the fields. They held each other. The smell of beans and hocks on the woodstove filled the two-room cabin and drifted onto the porch. Tom smiled at his Chloe. "It sure was good of masta Shelby to give us dem hocks, it sho make a difference."

Chloe smiled and replied, "All you do round here, you deserve 'em more'n anybody, specially Clyde."

"Baby, he my boss and masta's right hand, of course he gonna eat good, that how it goes." Tom kissed Chloe on the head as the silhouettes of their two boys rose in the distance.

Clyde the overseer stopped his horse in front of the porch. He looked down at the pair, then looked over his shoulder at the approaching twins "Looks like you got this thing all worked out, boy," Clyde said to Tom, still looking toward the boys.

"We do our best, Mr. Clyde. you care to stay fo' suppa?"

The overseer sat tall on his horse and looked down at the two on the porch step. He smiled and rode towards his own cabin. As soon as the overseer was out of earshot Chloe slapped Tom playfully on his arm and rolled her eyes. Tom smiled. "It ain't his fault he ain't got nobody."

"It's exactly his fault, he mean and spiteful. You can see it in his eyes. One day all that poison gonna spill out all over the place," she said.

The next morning Tom and his boys were heading into the field long before the sun had a chance to rise. The rest of the field slaves would follow soon. Tom and his boys would open the tool shed and prepare the curing barn so no time would be wasted. By dawn Chloe was preparing breakfast in the main house for master Shelby and his family.

The sun was strong by the time Clyde rode into the fields. Tom mended a tobacco sled as Enos split wood for the furnace. Elbert led a mule pulling a full sled of tobacco, arriving at the curing barn the same time as Clyde.

"Why ain't the furnace stoked yet, ya'll got leaves already."

Enos replied while gathering an arm load of kindling. "-Bout to be suh."

"Tom, do you like bein' headman?" asked Clyde.

"Yes, suh," Tom answered, his nerves lighting up because he could smell the liquor on Clyde.

"Then show a little more get up, boy."

"Yes, suh. We give it our all, suh." said Tom.

Elbert stared at Clyde while gathering the lugs from the sled. "I'll bet you do boy, I'll bet you do," Clyde said, almost to himself. As he turned to ride away he locked eyes with Elbert, who kept working without looking away. Clyde spat his tobacco and continued into the fields. Tom noticed the interaction and his pulse quickened as he shouted, "Elbert! Get on back out there!"

As evening settled on the fields Tom washed himself from a barrel behind the shack. Chloe cooked her fourth meal of the day, the first for her and her family. Out of breath and wild, Enos came running into the tiny cabin, startling Chloe.

"Elbert gone! Elbert gone!" he shouted as Chloe tried to understand what he was yelling about.

Tom came up the porch and asked, "What you on about, boy?"

"Elbert gone! Ain't no one seen him since this afternoon! I been up and down the crops and nothin'!"

Tom and Chloe stood puzzling at Enos as the sound of horses coming up the road grew louder. Tom turned and gasped. Chloe and Enos rushed to the porch and stopped dead next to Tom. Clyde brought his horse to a stop in front of the cabin. Elbert was bound at the wrists and leashed to the saddle by a six-foot lead. He was badly beaten. It was obvious he'd been partly dragged home. The blood on his swollen face was a sticky dust color. His clothes were torn open. Enos sprang for his brother but Tom had a powerful, lightning-fast grip on him.

Clyde proclaimed, "Caught the boy tryin' to run. I'm takin' him to the box and Shelby willdecide what to do with all of ya in the morn'!" Enos broke free of Tom's grip and ran to his brother. Two men on horseback that nobody had noticed came down hard on Enos with bull whips. Tom screamed"-Stop! Stop it!" but stood still on the porch as Chloe rushed to gather Enos. The two strangers got a few more licks in on both Enos and his mother. Clyde grinned and tipped his hat to Tom.

The morning found Tom and Enos standing at the bottom of master Shelby's large porch."I must protect my family, Tom. You understand that as well as anybody. This farm is all we got, and I must protect it no matter what."

Tom's eyes had not lifted from the ground since master Shelby came out from his breakfast and began talking. Shelby stood atop his porch talking down at his property. Tom leveled his gaze at his master's polished leather boots and tried to speak."No way my boy tried to—"

"Careful Tom, Clyde is a God-fearing, white Christian, and I'm bound to trust his word."

Clyde stood at the bottom of the staircase, one step above Tom and smiled down at him. "I'll arrange it so Elbert goes somewhere he'll be happy, more productive. I got young ones too, Tom. I know how precocious they can be when they're not challenged. Besides, I can get three in trade for him. By the grace of God he's strong like you Tom but seems he ain't got the common sense you do." Chloe listened from behind the screen door of the house, biting her lip as tears ran. Miss Shelby whispered in Chloe's ear "We only want what's best for you and your family."

Tom woke up in the yard with his head splitting. Feeling his blood-crusted scalp obliterated the dream. He remembered master Ian. He struggled to his knees. He squinted at the sun. Looking into his bloody hands he remembered the smoke rising from master Ian's hair. He vomited. Between retching he yelled for Lily. He cried for his boys and long-lost wife. It would be the last time he cried out loud. After some time, out of bile and out of breath, Tom knew she was gone. Lily, Chloe, his boys, all of them gone.

He walked into town to get help. He frightened everyone who saw him. His disfigured face contorted in pain. His whole body covered in blood. By noon the sheriff and his men had decided old, simple Tom had turned on Ian. They ignored his story. They credited his cracked and swollen skull to Ian. Their own fear explained everything they needed to know. By dusk there was a capture or kill bounty issued for the two missing slaves. The next day, old Tom hung charred and smoking from the southern live oak in the town square.

67

CHAPTER 9

The Boy

The mangrove beach was an orchestra of animal sounds in the pre-dawn. The bugs and birds and frogs sang to the sunrise. Lily dug into the sand amongst the low, naked scrub brush for concealment in the daylight. She showed the Boy how to pull the sand toward him and then push it away to either side. He moved slow, not interested in hiding. Lily did the work unconsciously. She was desperate to conjure a plan. She had no idea where to go next, only a vague direction to run when night fell. They were in a hole of sand and grass and agreed if they were still and silent they could spend the day in safety. The sand was cool, and it soothed Lily's aches. Sleep came fast.

Soaked through with sweat the Boy startled awake. The molded sand had a firm grip on him. He wanted to cry out but felt Lily next to him. Focused on his predicament he almost did not notice the people on the beach. At the water's edge were three black men and a boat. The men were talking but he could not hear what they were saying until one of them turned to him and said,"Let's go!"

The man motioned for him to get on the boat. He tried not to move, not to breath. How could the man see him. Didn't he know they were fugitives, trying to escape to somewhe-re, to freedom? Lily felt a grip on her shoulder. Breathless she opened her eyes expecting the worst. There was nobody standing above her, only the Boy lying next to her, squeezing hard. She noticed he was stiff with fear and followed his eyes to the three men next to the boat. She reached to him for mutual assurance and he moved his head just enough to look her in the eyes. His look implored"What do we do?" With her eyes she said,"stay still."

That's when everything exploded. All around them the brush came alive with arms and legs and feet, all rushing through the brush. He and Lily held their breath as they got stepped over, stepped on, and kicked. Sand filled their eyes and ears. The Boy's nose bled but they remained silent. The man that had given the blow to the Boy's face paused and looked back as he regained his footing in the soft sand. The stranger held his and Lily's gaze for a moment with a kind of recognition in his eyes. He turned and continued onto the boat without a word or second look. It was the biggest of the original three men that noticed the man's pause. When he finally found the eyes of the two half-buried fugitives, he waved them to the boat. When they did not budge, he shouted, "Let's go, now, or we'll leave you behind!"

The birds and frogs and crickets were no longer singing. The sun was strong. The big man sauntered through the sand as everyone else climbed aboard. The Boy and Lily had not moved a single muscle. As the man approached, they grew even more impossibly still.

He knelt beside the twisted bramble and cowering bodies. He spoke with a calm and caring tone. "I'm taking all these people somewhere safe. Somewhere they can be free, without no one chasing them." Dead silence prompted the man to start again.

"I know you scared right now but remember where you at. Still close to the masta's house, still within reach of the dogs and the noose." The man stood. "If it's freedom you want then come with me and my friends. But if you want to keep running, or to die, then this is a good place as any."

Lily did not move; she did not speak. When the Boy opened his mouth she let out a small sound that screamed for him to shut up. He ignored her and asked the man where the boat was going.

"An island," he said.

"Who are those people?"

"People like you. People who want to be free."

He asked the man why he would want to help."Because those people are my people, our people, and we all need to look after each other." With that he walked back to the boat. The Boy stood up and tried to wipe the sticky sand from his bloody face and sweaty clothes and ran after the man.

"No!" Lily cried out. He did not listen. Lily picked herself up like she was lifting the weight of the world. Through tears and sweat and sand, she staggered towards the blurry boat.

CHAPTER 10

The Island

The boat was black with soot, as if it had been pulled from a long-dead fire pit. The Boy and Lily stood on the deck not knowing what to do next. The big man asked them to remain topside with him. Looking down into the hold of the boat they could only see terrified eyes staring back. The Boy only guessed what"topside" meant and sat next to Lily. He tried to spit the sand from his mouth. Lily stared down into her leathery hands and sweat-stained lap, trying to brush away the sand.

The three men began speaking to each other about tides and currents. Things the Boy had only vague ideas about. Two of the men used long wooden poles to move the boat away from the beach into deeper water. The big man stood firm at the helm. When the boat pointed toward another gnarled forest of mangrove the two men began to work in earnest. They pushed the boat along on either side. They worked hard, and the heavy boat rocked from side to side as each man took his turn, sometimes in unison sometimes not.

The morning was already hot and the air thick with moisture. Everything onboard seemed soaked to its core. One tall mast stood bare and wet near the center of the short, wide deck. Another shorter mast rose from the rear of the boat. Rope ran from the sides and front of the boat to the top of each mast. From these hung various flags, most so tattered that they were unrecognizable, their symbols and meanings gone to the wind. The big man told the world in front of him, in a booming voice, "Stay quiet! If we want to get past these shallow bays and mangroves we got to be as inconspicuous as possible."

The Boy noticed something about the man when he used the word "inconspicuous." There was a slight change in posture that said the big man was proud to use the word. He also noticed the two men working with the poles steal a quick glance and fleeting grin at each other. The transient grins frightened him, he felt contempt in them and wanted to tell the big man. The big man's pride made him feel a tiny bit safer. He could relate to the feeling; he'd felt it many times himself. He looked at Lily and felt her silence. It made him wonder if she was still there.

As the last of the thick mangroves lay behind the boat the men could no longer touch bottom with the poles. They stowed the poles and began pulling thick piles of canvas from the front of the boat. They attached these mounds of canvas to the wooden masts one at a time. In a matter of minutes the sails were up and full of a fresh breeze. The big man lowered a long plank from the right side of the boat, tied it secure, and returned to the wheel. All three men relaxed in their posture. As the boat rolled slightly to one side each man took a seat. One at the front and one at the back.

The big man at the wheel sat back against his bench and studied the small canvas sails. The Boy knew from reading that he was sailing, but never did any of those books with all those words explain this feeling of exhilaration. He was grinning ear to ear. The big man turned to look back, and he too was smiling. "If you've ever wondered what it means to be free, well, this is just about it," the man said.

The horizon was wide open and endless. No mangroves, no trees, no land, and somehow this made the Boy's whole body swoon.

"Freedom," he whispered to himself. He wondered about the word and how it related to this feeling. It didn't make sense. He wanted to ask the big man, but he agreed that there must be some correlation. He felt unbound, alive. Lily finally lifted her eyes to the horizon, a tiny hope growing.

As darkness fell the boat became a little livelier. The big man remained at the helm as the other two began passing water down to the people in the hold. "My name is Ras," the big man said to the Boy and Lily. "I'm in charge here on the boat and fourth in command at home." Ras was so calm that it seemed to affect whomever he would interact with. Hearing him speak made the Boy relax. Lily remained skeptical but had less of a grip on herself.

"It's an island paradise. Got everything a man needs to thrive in this world. Many of us have made it our home and made it fruitful. The two of you could be valuable, I can see you are intelligent. If you are willing you both could become pillars of our little paradise. You will see for yourselves, but I think you both will be a good fit. If you want to be free our leader will show you how, as he's shown me and many others."

The Boy reveled at the idea of being a free man, although deep inside he had so many questions. He felt conflicted. He believed he was already free, at least as free as a black person could be. He made his own decisions as well as he could, but he also knew that he needed some things decided for him. He knew that God made black people slaves for a reason.

He could see details in the dark. The reflection of the moon, and the wind on the water. The invigorating smell of salt and decay was heavy in the air. His adrenaline had come and gone so many times today that he could barely keep his eyes open. He tried his best to stay awake. Instinctively he knew that it might be dangerous to sleep. Lily watched Ras pilot the boat as she held him and wondered about their future. She would not let herself believe they were heading for anything good, but a tiny ember of hope burned deep inside.

As soon as the boat hit the beach the men were shouting, pulling people from the hold one by one. Most of the passengers had been sick during the trip. Everyone below was covered in the stench. Rising from the guts of the boat they had trouble seeing in the sunlight. They fell more than climbed down to the soft sand. They mostly lay still where they fell until the shouting started again. "Get up! Move to the water and wash yourselves!"

The dozen or so people moved towards the water, some still retching. The Boy and Lily were the last off the boat except for Ras; he stood tall in the cockpit observing the scene on the beach. As the Boy helped Lily down and turned to climb down himself, he caught eyes with Ras. Ras smiled and resumed overseeing the cargo as they struggled in the shore break. As soon as the Boy's feet touched the ground his stomach started turning. He was seasick and began dry heaving his empty stomach. The ground pitched and rolled under him.

He tried to sit still, wishing the feeling away. He stared at his boots. On the boat he noticed Ras and the other two wore beautiful boots. They looked like they were made from alligator. He felt lucky to have his own boots now that he was free.

His throat burned. He looked out over the expanse of water stretching to the horizon. At the water's edge he knelt to drink, careful not to get too close. He felt afraid of the water, unsure why. A couple gulps and he vomited again.

The men, women, and a few children lay strewn about the beach, clean from the ocean and now dry from the sun. Most of them slept. The Boy watched Lily sleep as he began to notice where he was. The beach was wide and sloped down towards the sea. The sand was powdery soft and almost white. A couple of yards behind him the jungle was thick and impenetrable, making a straight line in both directions as far as he could see. The sky was cloudless.

Crusty salt residue stained his skin. Dry sand fell away from his body. As he brushed it away, he wondered what would come next. For a moment he wondered if it had been a mistake to get on the boat, but decided it was a good thing. He knew Lily was lost and unsure of where to go. He thought back to the feeling of sailing, the sun setting into the sea. He smiled to himself and remembered that he was free now. He could have anything, but all he wanted was food and water. He hoped the men who brought them here would give them something to drink.

Yelling erupted from the jungle line, as group of white men on horses came fast onto the beach. They all carried whips and made them crack while shouting out commands. The Boy froze, wide-eyed. He watched the others scramble to their feet and try to obey. He and Lily followed suit. The startled group was ordered to form a line. Some of the slaves were slow to join and they tasted the sharp bite of a whip followed by more yelling. At least half of them were crying out, some in pain, some in fear. When the men shouted at them to shut up, some ceased crying and some felt more of the flesh tearing whip.

When the group was silent the men on horseback moved towards the jungle line and stood, fearsome. The Boy tried with his eyes to speak with Ras, but the man sneered at the group. A moment later a pure white man, white hair, white eyebrows, dressed in all black like a preacher, on a white horse, emerged from the jungle. The strange-looking man eyed the crowd, sizing up everyone for a long time. When he lifted his gaze toward the horizon his eyes seemed to lock onto something in the distance.

The Boy stole a glance up at the man. Curious, he turned to see what the man was staring at and found a ship just visible on the horizon. When he turned back the man was staring straight at him. He averted his eyes to the sand in front of him, like the rest of the slaves. He knew enough to be frightened. When he finally stole another glance up, the man had resumed scanning the crowd. The Boy began breathing again.

After a few more minutes the man spoke. His voice was loud without shouting. It rose above the small surf crashing on the beach and the cacophony of sea birds.

"You are here because you desire to be free! Yet none of you understand what that means. Few white men know what that means let alone you of the savage, Godless races. Perhaps you saw your previous masters as captors, or worse. This only reinforces my belief that the mud races are too ignorant to understand the nuanced and complex nature that is a free man. God forgives your ignorance as I forgive your ignorance. But as God's grace is everlasting, mine is not! I expect you to learn, I expect you to relinquish your selfish heathen ways. I expect you to strive to become, if not a civilized God-fearing man, at least a well-behaved and obedient supplicant of God. We are all soldiers of the Almighty."

"Some of us are put here to lead and some to follow, but we must all do our part. To know your place is to begin on the path to freedom. To act as a fully formed human being, or at least mimic the greater race is to begin on the path to freedom. To develop a modicum of discipline of the self is to begin on the path to freedom. Some of you will learn this, some of you may not. Those that do will thrive, those that do not will surely suffer and most likely perish. This is not entirely up to you because of your not fully formed brain, but I will certainly take this into consideration. All you really need to do is try. All that I expect of you is effort, effort, and obedience."

The man gestured with an outstretched arm. "These fine examples that brought you here have proven themselves to possess uncommon effort. They are as close as the lesser races can get to a fully formed, God-fearing human. They will be your example. Follow their orders and you will begin to grow further from the animal state, and closer to God."

The man scanned the crowd for another minute. Then he raised his face to the sky and stretched both arms wide. He closed his eyes and began shouting gibberish to the heavens. As he grew louder the Boy began to feel like he didn't want to be here anymore. He felt like he'd made a mistake. The shouting stopped. The man turned his horse and disappeared into the jungle. The white men followed. Ras and the other two began shouting all over again.

The footpath was a narrow, single track cut through dense jungle. The canopy blocked out the sky. After about a mile the path opened onto a large meadow. On one side of the clearing were rows of tiny, handmade huts lined up in perfect symmetry. There were three rows of thirty, and more being built on either end. Each had four walls and a flat roof. Not tall enough for a grown man to stand up straight and just long and wide enough for two to lie down side by side. On the other side of the field was a large barn, big enough to hold a hundred head of cattle.

Past the buildings were perfect rows of tobacco as far as the Boy could see. He'd seen raw tobacco before on some of the plantations he'd visited with master Conner. A pang of sorrow ripped through him. He remembered standing on a porch listening to master Conner visit with the people she had come to see. As he'd gazed out over the fields of tobacco, he'd watched the slaves bent to their work. They wore little and what they did have on was stained with sweat. Their faces, the faces he could see from this distance, wore no expression, they were stone faced. He remembered looking down at his polished shoes and felt a kind of joy. Happy to be on the porch and not in the fields, happy to be wearing the fine clothes and leather shoes. He was joyful to be in such a good position for a slave, too important to pick crops in a field under a hot sun.

His memories were trampled by more men on horses and more yelling. This time the men were black, and he noticed they all wore the same alligator boots. Ras began yelling instructions. The group stared at the scene in front of them with disbelief. It looked like a thousand slaves working amongst the large leafy crops. Some were starting to understand that they had not escaped at all. A few seemed confused. Most wore heartbreak on their faces.

The men and women were separated. Anyone under teenage years was also split from the group. This caused some of the men and women to start howling and the men with whips jumped to action. The entire group watched a distraught woman fight hard to keep her daughter with her. She was so ferocious that two men had to abandon the whips as they beat her unconscious. She lay crumpled in the mud of her own blood and body fluids as the three groups were taken their separate ways. The Boy watched Lily walk away without looking back at him. She looked much older somehow, bent closer to the ground. She walked slow. He couldn't help but blame her for this terrible mistake.

His group received instructions on where to sleep and when to report to work. His insides twisted and tore apart. He thought back to the scene in the mangroves and wished with everything inside of him that he could go back there. The next instant his mind jumped to home, to the yard, to Tom, to master Ian. He remembered Lily's panic. He could hear Tom and Lily arguing. He remembered agreeing with old Tom. He ached to be back there with Tom, to side with Tom and make Lily see the truth. He felt venom towards the woman who'd forced him to leave home. But worst of all, for the first time in his brief life, he felt alone.

The group of men were marched to the edge of a large field of tobacco plants. There were at least twenty men in the field bent to their work already.

Ras reached down and pulled a leaf from the nearest plant. "You boys is just in time for the beginning of harvest. This here is tobacco. This is a lug, it's the bottom leaves. These is what you will be picking. Snap it off at the stalk so you don't hurt the rest of the plant."

With a great deal of physical emphasis, he showed the group of men the leaf and explained how to separate the leaf from the plant. He warned about the potential to destroy the entire plant if it were done wrong. "You will see some of us on horses, we will be helping you work. If you got any questions raise up your hand."

The Boy raised his hand and between sobs managed to whisper, "I work in the house, sir."

Ras replied to the group, "You free men now. This is a chance to improve yo' self. Hard work, not women's work, will make you men. Free men."

Then he smiled wide and pointed up and behind the group. They turned in unison and caught sight of the object. In the canopy of the dense jungle hung a figure, not human but human-like. They looked harder and realized, again almost in unison, that it was in fact a human torso. It hung from a rope around the neck and had its arms and legs removed. It had also been burnt beyond recognition. "Leave if you want. But if you stay, don't cause no trouble and be sho' to keep yo' mind on yo' work. If you lucky you might understand what Boss was tellin' you!"

The men fled into the field and began picking leaves. The Boy stood frozen, staring at the odd, burnt, half of a body. Most of the men had seen such things for most of their lives, he had not. He cried out loud. The bull whip cut fast into his back, snapping him from his horror. As he realized he was standing alone he quickly disappeared into the field of tobacco.

Daylight faded. The field cleared of men. The newly arrived fell into line with the group as they moved like ghosts towards a common haunting. The men on horseback were gone. A bonfire in the next clearing came into view together with the smell of something savory. The Boy thought of the hanged torso and tried to push it away. He thought of his aching feet and was grateful for his boots. He wondered where Lily was. He yearned for home. He began to tear up as he followed the men.

At the fire, a fat, bare-chested man handed each man a bowl filled with something from a boiling cauldron. They sat in the grass eating with their fingers. When the Boy took his first mouthful he gagged. Starving, he tried again. His belly roiled as he sat in the grass watching the group of men eat. By the time he finished, the rest of the men had dispersed. When there were only a few lonely figures left, mostly men from the boat, he began to wonder where he would sleep. He wondered about Lilly. *Where was she right now? Where would she sleep? Had she eaten the same rotten slop? Had she seen the torso?* His stomach jumped at the thought and he threw up everything. On his hands and knees, his boots digging into the soft ground, his guts heaved until not even saliva came out.

He woke with the warm sun on his face. He sat upright and smiled at the familiar barn and grand house beyond. A sharp kick to the head snatched him from his dream. He huddled into a defensive position. He noticed it was still dark as he took another kick to the body, then blows began striking fast and hard on him. It seemed as if feet and fists were falling out of the sky like rain.

Warm blood choked him awake. This time there was light on the horizon and men walking past him. Rolling over and spitting out blood he knew he should get up and join the group. His first attempt to stand was a failure. A man on a horse cut into his back with a whip and he bounced up like a spring. He walked hunched over. He breathed shallow. He made it all the way to the tobacco field before he noticed his bare feet and missing shirt. He teared up over his favorite boots. He realized someone had beaten him and stole them during the night. The stench of shit and piss filled his nostrils and he discovered that he had soiled himself. Bent low and sobbing, he began to pick the bright, broad leaves.

CHAPTER 11

New Orleans
The Conners

James Conner and his daughter Elizabeth arrived in New Orleans looking for a new start. But the malevolent guilt of survival clung to each of them like a shadow.

Stepping off the coach, Elizabeth gazed wide-eyed at the bustle. Looking back at her father crushed her enthusiasm. James had devoted himself to the ghosts of Sara and Josephine along with the false story of the illness. This was all that young Elizabeth could see when she looked at her father.

James surveyed the busy city center with contempt. Everywhere he looked he saw black faces, slaves and free alike. Thoughts of yellow fever threatened the air he breathed. He unconsciously covered his mouth and nose with his handkerchief. He choked out orders for Elizabeth to stay close. He squeezed her tiny hand too hard, dragging her into the New Orleans office of the New American Shipping Company.

James purchased a large stone house with an imposing iron gate. Three slaves, included in the price of the house, remained to cook, clean, and tend to the stable and horses. James struggled with not wanting them in the house and needing them to do the work. He rarely uttered a word to them. When he caught Elizabeth talking to one of them, he would turn red and shuffle her off to another room. He'd explain, "It was your mother's proximity to negroes that killed her and your sister!" He would repeat this sentiment often. He went as far as explaining how years ago back in Ireland, two negroes had tried to kill his own mother and brother. He knew that it was a lie, but he believed the exaggeration was necessary to keep Elizabeth safe.

By the time Elizabeth was sixteen she had seen countless public displays of violence in the name of "taming" the negro. She had also seen violent outbursts from the "un-tamed." She didn't remember her mother's fierce resistance to the idea that blacks were other than human. She believed her father.

At a live performance of "The Hunters of Kentucky," James pointed out a free negro couple in the audience. They sat third row center, dressed in the latest fashion. "They're only pretending to mimic the ways of civilized people. If pushed or challenged, they will quickly revert back to the barbarians they are. They have been taught by a far too extravagant republic. Some of them might be smart enough for this sort of indoctrination but in their hearts they remain incapable of understanding virtue or believing in the one true God."

By twenty Elizabeth knew that any races with skin darker than an Italian, for instance, were inferior. If dark enough, Italians and Spanish should be included.

Elizabeth fell in love. She married Craven McInnis, a man fresh off the boat from the old world, like her father. But unlike her father, Craven came from poor beginnings. His mother fled Ireland with her newborn during the lead-up to the Orange Order. His father was killed by the Peep o' Day Boys at Loughgal four months before he was born.

Craven grew up in the brothels of London and eventually Amsterdam, where his mother finally died of a fondness for gin and opium.

He made his way onto a Dutch slaver at fourteen. By sixteen he had travelled through West Africa, Brazil, and the Caribbean. At seventeen Craven landed in the port of New Orleans with all the enthusiasm of the new world. He deserted the slave ship along with its supremacist ideas and fell in love with Elizabeth.

He was popular with James during the courtship. James reminisced about Ireland and Craven shared stories of England and the meaner streets of Holland. Elizabeth thrilled at seeing her father smile for the first time she could remember.

They were married in the spring. The newlyweds shared the big house with James. Craven resisted but Elizabeth insisted. Craven was handsome and charming, but he was a dreamer. He was comfortable with hard work, but labor was cheap. James had trouble understanding how a young man struggled to find his way in such a prosperous country. He too often shared the story of how he landed in New York sick to death with nothing but a few coins in his pocket. "I had no one to trust but managed to become rich despite the cruel world."

Elizabeth listened with eager eyes, sure that her father's initiative would rub off on Craven. The only other story James Conner told over and over usually signaled the end of dinner. "The blacks tried to kill my family back in Ireland. They succeeded in killing my whole family here."

During this second speech Elizabeth would gaze toward Craven with down-turned eyes, never looking at him directly. She hoped the story would help persuade him to their way of thinking about race, the correct way. Craven's world view showed him that people were people and that the color of skin was of no more import than the color of eyes.

The opulent mahogany dinner table began to grow into a stone rampart between two warring factions, with Elizabeth stranded on top.

She would always choose her father. By the time Ian was born Craven and Elizabeth slept in separate rooms. Craven nurtured a whiskey bottle and opium eventually defeated his lust for other women. Elizabeth tried to nurture her baby but found only resentment in the effort. The house became three separate dwellings.

A sultry August evening found Craven standing in the study, face to face with James Conner's recently commissioned self-portrait, a gift from Elizabeth. The fireplace was cold, the only sound was the dinner table being set in the next room. Craven chuckled to himself as he fumbled with the flintlock blunderbuss and thought, *A better story for the old man to ruin dinner with.*

Elizabeth changed her name back to Conner against custom. She detested the thought of being associated with the weakness of suicide. She shared her feelings of disgust with young Ian about his father's weakness often and with vigor. When her father died, she demanded her three slaves call her"Master" instead of"Mistress." She hardened inside like a fossil.

CHAPTER 12

The Island

A full season of working the tobacco fields made the Boy strong. His skin became tight and dark. His bare feet became hard and callused. He forgot about his boots. He claimed shelter in one of the small bare huts lined up at the edge of the field. He shared it with another man whom he had not spoken to beyond threats of violence. He knew he was lying, the man did not. He slept, but his dreams were still consumed by thoughts of home, and master Conner.

When he thought of Lily, which was less and less lately, his stomach would drop realizing he hadn't heard or seen her since that first day. He wondered where she was, what she was doing. He kept looking for her in the fields, but she never appeared.

He scolded her in his mind for putting them in this hellish place. *I should have never got on the boat. I should have never listened to her. She forced us to leave home. I got on the boat to make a bad situation better. Her overreaction to master*

Ian's accident put us in danger. I know it was an accident and Lily left Tom to help by himself. She dragged me into the night not knowing where she was going or even why. She chose a dangerous place to hide in that woman's barn. That woman had every right to shoot us both for trespassing. After weeks of putting his mind to it he realized that it was Lily that had got them to this awful place.

The work was simple. The first couple of months they picked top buds and suckers, always on the lookout for hornworms. He worked in silence. He got used to the men on horseback riding along the fields, watching. Ras was one of those men. Ras never spoke a word to him after the first day. When the Boy recognized Ras, he refused to look at the man. He put his anger into the work. He fantasized about hurting Ras. Exhaustion turned the anger to sadness. Betrayal crept in and he thought of Lily. This was his routine.

During harvest the bottom leaves, or lugs, as Ras had called them, got picked and piled onto sleds. Pulling the sleds to the barn reminded him of Tom's horses. Sometimes he would make horse noises to himself and laugh. Sometimes he noticed muscles he never knew he had. Sometimes he thought of his old life and the burning in his stomach would creep up to his chest, then up to his eyes, then spill out and down his cheeks.

The pickaxe was heavy at first. It ripped open his callused hands and the earth at the same time. By the second week of plowing with the pickaxe his new calluses had grown thick.

His hands stopped bleeding. The tool had become his favorite. He could use it with ease, sometimes choking up and using it with one hand, clearing stones with the other. He liked the feeling he got when he finished a row ahead of the others.

The Boy stood in line for his meal. A man on horseback came trotting into the clearing. When the man and beast came close enough to one of the bonfires he recognized him as Ras. His heart leapt and he wondered why he cared at all. It was Ras who had tricked him onto the boat. It was Ras who had been nice to him and then did nothing to help him when they got to this place. He understood that Ras was just like Lily. They'd both tricked him; they both had used him to get something for themselves. That's when he realized why he hadn't seen Lily in the fields. She was living in luxury in the master's house and she hadn't bothered to send for him. The anger was hot in his chest as he ignored Ras's approach.

Ras looked down from his horse. "Hey, boy! Field work got you deaf?"

The Boy tried harder to ignore him. He looked the other way. He looked at the ground. The line of men before and behind him had made a large space, cowering away from the man and his horse. The Boy was alone and exposed.

"Come on with me, boy. I got something to show you."

He could only think of how Ras had sounded just before he got on the boat. Tears welled up hot in his eyes and his heart tried to jump out of his chest. Ras reached a hand down and repeated himself. Without looking up the Boy moved toward the horse and took Ras's hand. He was startled at how willing he was to go with this man who had betrayed him. Ras's grip was strong and in that instant he was up onto the beast behind Ras. He stopped crying and held tight.

A short ride found them at a new bonfire where other men were eating. These men sat at long narrow tables using forks and knives. A half dozen horses stood stoic in a corral near the edge of light. Another fat man stood near another large black caldron and dished out bowls of food to these men too. They dismounted and approached the line. The Boy wiped his eyes and began to see that the grill had large pieces of meat on it. Potatoes and green vegetables shared space on the grate over the fire. That's when the smell hit and he almost fainted.

"Whoa, take it easy, boy. You pass out and you can't eat." Ras held the Boy's shoulders and looked him in the eyes. "We gonna sit down and eat like men but first you gotta show me that you is a man."

When he nodded in agreement Ras smiled a big warm smile. Between the heat from the fire, the aroma from the cooking meat and the warm approving smile from Ras, his knees went weak again. This time he hit the ground.

He came to, hearing a soft roar of laughter and feeling a steel-like grip on his arm lifting him to his feet. He blushed hot for a moment and tried hard to steady himself. Ras led him around the back side of the cook camp. When he finally let go, they were standing in front of a short, thin man sitting on his haunches peeling potatoes. The Boy looked down at the man and the man smiled back then looked further up towards Ras with a questioning gaze. The man was so skinny he looked sickly, the Boy thought.

Ras spoke."You a man or a boy?" He looked up at Ras with a similar look on his face as the man with the potatoes.

"Are you a man or a boy?" Ras repeated.

"I'm a man, sir."

All three were stone still."A man or a boy?" Ras yelled.

"A man!" The Boy yelled back, surprising himself and the man in front of him.

Ras laughed."Because only men get to eat at these tables. Only men can work with me. Do you want to work with me boy?"

"Yes!"

"Then a man gotta prove it. A man gotta show hisself and everybody around him that he is a man. You ready to do that?"

The Boy's brain moved fast as he answered"Yes" again but he could not understand what was being asked of him.

The skinny man's face changed from questioning to concerned and he diverted his eyes to the potatoes. The Boy recognized that all the men on the other side of the cook camp were watching him. Ras shook him. "Forget about them and pay close attention."

He half turned and looked up at Ras. Ras pointed to the ground, and he followed his finger. His gaze landed on something out of place but familiar. *My boots*, he said to himself.

The boots on the potato man's feet were his. The Boy's first thought was how good his feet felt because of not wearing boots for the past several months. He also wondered how such a sickly-looking man could have had the power to beat him that night. Still unsure of what was being asked of him he turned to look at Ras. The potato man rose, dropping the potatoes and adjusting his grip on the small knife he was peeling with. Ras struck the man, knocking him to the ground. The Boy backed away a few steps and froze.

"This ain't the time to run away, boy. You need to lean into this if you want to be a man." Picking up the small knife, Ras kept one foot on the downed man's chest, and reached the knife out to the Boy. A small relief passed over him as he assumed that it was peeling potatoes, his new job, that Ras was pushing him into. But the look in Ras's eyes grew dangerous. The Boy sensed there was something else he wanted.

"Take this and tend to yo' business. You got this one chance to be a man, to be in charge, to be free!"

His heart fluttered and the ringing in his ears drowned out the silence of the men watching. "If you don't take this knife I will drop it and let this man up and the rest will be what it be. Not good for you, I suppose."

The Boy met eyes with the man on his back and the sinister grin on the man's face caused him to take another step back. Ras sighed "I was counting on you to be my main man. I thought for sure you would be smart enough to work by my side. I guess I was wrong."

He lifted his boot off the potato man. He dropped the knife at the Boy's feet. He turned to the men watching and shook his head as he walked back to the group. The potato man sprang onto the knife and then onto the Boy, knocking him to the ground. Focused on the knife, the Boy somehow grabbed hold of the man's wrists. A few seconds felt like an hour as he wondered at the skinny man's strength. A few more seconds passed, and he stood panting. The potato man was lying flat on his back digging his boot heels into the black earth and making an awful noise. Blood sputtered from a large rip in his throat as he tried to put the tear back together. Time stopped. He lay quiet. No more gurgling and sputtering, no more squirming.

The roar of the crowd snapped time back into motion. The Boy looked at the knife in his hand and let it go as if he were setting it free. He tried to wipe the smell of rusted iron from his nostrils but his bloody hands made it worse. He looked down at his own torso soaked in blood and began to gag.

The next instant he was at the table of men. They saluted him with deafening noise and slaps on the back, and an awful-tasting drink. They fed him. Soon he was singing along with them.

Dawn hadn't broken yet as the hammer in his head smashed him. At first it was a dream; The Boy followed the cat into the barn and on a soft, broken bale of hay, he sat down with the cat. It purred on his lap. It rubbed its whiskers on the boy. The purring got louder. It kneaded its claws into the Boy's thigh. The purring got louder. The cat licked the Boy and at the same time he felt the cat's claws digging into his neck. Blood ran hot down his chest. He tried to pull the cat off, but the claws dug deeper. The Boy tried to stand but he had an unbearable weight on his shoulders. The cat sat in front of the Boy and hissed a terrible, stinking blackness. The Boy had a hammer in his hand and began hitting the cat. He hammered relentlessly on the old barn cat. The cat made a disgusting noise and squirmed in the dirt. As the Boy's arm began to ache the cat would be still and silent. A moment later the old cat would be purring loud in his lap again. With tears in his eyes, and blood everywhere he repeated the nightmare over and over.

The hammer was in his head now. Banging inside his head like nothing he'd ever known. It was still dark when he rolled over and began to puke. He fell from the large tabletop and landed face first on the cold ground. He continued to puke.

Catching his breath, he heard a horse approaching in the half-light. The horse and rider stopped just shy of trampling him as he cowered and thought of his strange dream. He was struck by something hard and heavy followed by a soft but serious voice."Pick it up and drink. You gonna need some water. This here might be the most important day of your life."

He found the canteen and tried to put out the fire in his throat."Get up," Ras said as he turned his horse and headed into the day. The Boy struggled to his feet. He followed, clutching the canteen to his bloodstained chest.

"I understand yo' problem, boy. You feel like you in a worse place than before. Maybe you feel like I tricked you back on that beach."

The Boy staggered alongside the horse trying to focus on what Ras was saying."You have a chance to change everything today. You showed some grit last night and opened up some opportunity fo' yo' self."

The Boy's mind reeled through the fog of last night. He remembered blurry songs, stinging beer, roasted vegetables, and good meat. He flashed on the hammer and the cat in his dream. Then he remembered scattered potatoes and the sickening noise as the man squirmed in the dirt. He began puking all the water he'd drunk. He puked until nothing came up, then he caught his breath and looked up at Ras. Tears ran down his face.

"I know you been taught that what you done last night is wrong, a sin, but there is always a price to pay to become a man, a free man. Think about not doing nothing and staying bent over in them tobacco fields. Sleeping on the ground with a dirty slave next to you. Think about what that's going to look like in ten, twenty years. You still young but if you been paying any attention to those people around you they young too. They will die in those fields. You want to die that way?" Ras moved his horse forward. The Boy followed.

The path opened to a river. They stopped and watched the river move. "If you chose right you can work with me. Someday you can be up on a horse, you can be your own man, make your own decisions. You don't gotta be like those niggas in the field that choose to stay small and weak, waiting for us to feed them and take care of them."

The Boy didn't care about the words, he could only hear his own shame. "I was younger than you when I came here. I had seen all kinds of killin' and killed a man myself before I got here, so that part was easy. Trying to grasp the ideas that the Reverend was teaching me, or trying to teach me, that was the hard part. We only know what we know so there's no way to know what we don't know. Do you understand?" Ras stared down at the Boy. The Boy stared down at the ground.

"Doesn't matter right now. You'll figure it out. So here's the deal, you can decide to take charge of your life and work with me. Jump in that river and clean yo' self up and meet me back at camp for breakfast, or you can head on back to the fields.

Your choice. Just like life, you always got a choice." Ras turned his horse and without looking back added"So you know, that pot back at the field camp gets filled with whatever we kill. If you chose to go back be sure to tell everyone dinner is courtesy of you."

He watched Ras go as he fought back the horror. He stood silent for a moment then walked into the river. Even in August the river was cold and it stole his breath.

The walk back gave him time to talk himself into his decision. The choice was easy, believing in it was not. He told himself that he would die before returning to the fields. He had already killed a person, so going back made no sense. He assured himself that he did what he had to do to become a man, a free man according to Ras. But the conflict deep inside his gut remained strong and he argued with himself. *Yes, the man had taken my boots, or at least was wearing them. Did that mean he should die? Ras told me to kill the man and I did. How does that make me free? Or even a man?*

He looked down at his feet as he walked. The soft red dirt wasn't far from the color of his skin, and he liked how he blended with the earth. He thought of his old boots and how painful it would be to wear them. He wondered if they would even fit and knew right then he would never wear them again. His feet were strong with thick calluses. He questioned the need for shoes at all. He decided they were mostly for show, to fit in with other people with shoes, in places he had gone in his former life. He smiled at the thought of not needing shoes. He didn't need his old life, or his master, or Lily, especially Lily. She made him come here and then abandoned him. He told himself he didn't need anyone and felt lighter for it. He began to feel like a hero in some of the books he'd read. A man that could take care of himself, a dangerous man.

"I'm a man!" he shouted out loud. He ran the rest of the way back to his new camp.

His routine started before sunrise with the cook and the outdoor kitchen. The cook showed no feelings towards him. This surprised and confused him. He had killed the cook's helper and expected to feel a strong resentment. The cook only grumbled short instructions for a few days until a routine took hold. After that he never spoke again. The work was simple. The Boy became proficient fast. He felt his hands tremble and sweat every time he picked up the knife to peel potatoes.

As soon as the fire was strong and the raw food made ready to cook, he would move to the corral and prepare the horses for the men. Ras showed him how to saddle the horses the first morning, but the Boy resisted. He paid attention to everything but the horses.

The second morning came, and the horses were not ready. Ras walked him through the process again, this time with some mild violence. The Boy paid attention. He fed each a small pile of hay and as they ate he saddled them. This became his favorite part of the day. The horses warmed to him, and he swooned at the horse's reactions when they saw him coming. They would stomp in place and nicker, never taking their eyes off him. Sometimes they'd whinny if he was late or moving too slow. He felt something grow between him and the horses. He didn't know the word for it, but he liked the way they seemed to appreciate him. They would nuzzle him when he brushed them or comically show their teeth when they wanted more. He was starting to understand what Tom saw in the horses. He saw why the old man had spent so much time with them and talked with them as if they knew what he was saying. Taking care of the horses made him feel like a character in one of his books. He missed his books.

Walking the tobacco fields was the main job of the men. One or two men on horseback would ride on either side of the perimeter while one man walked inside the crops. The Boy remembered the view from inside the field, watching the men on horseback. He remembered trying not to look at the man on foot walking the rows with a long stick. The men removed bodies that had fallen dead where they worked. Or beat bodies that had fallen but still lived. The men called the dead bodies "sleepers." He would be one of those with the stick, walking the rows, removing the dead and beating the almost dead. He thought of the cat and the hammer. He shivered despite the morning sun.

Ras rode tall and explained the harvesting of tobacco, as if the Boy had not worked the fields every waking hour for over a year. The Boy followed on foot and noticed the pride beaming from Ras as he explained this and that. It became contagious as he watched more than listened. He felt a confidence being close to Ras. He felt stronger walking next to the horse. He felt pride looking at the saddle cinched down just right, the way it fit and held everything in place. Learning how to saddle a horse made him wonder what else he might be missing. He thought of the years watching Tom and why he'd never cared to learn.

He began to notice details about Ras. He realized that the men all wore the same clothes, light cotton trousers, a cotton shirt. They all wore the same boots made of leather and alligator. They were in uniform, and the Boy wondered if he would get to wear one.

"You hearin' me, boy?" Ras asked as he stopped his horse. He looked up smiling and nodded. Ras smiled back and continued talking"Reverend got a big operation. He grows a lot of different crops, but this part here, these few tobacco fields is mine to look after. Me and the boys, we in charge here. You with us now, so you gotta pay attention."

He looked up at Ras again. Ras sat even taller than before, and the Boy felt a certainty that he had never felt. Movement on the ridge behind Ras caught his eye. It was a white man on a horse, and he was watching them. He had a rifle. The certainty disappeared from the Boy's stomach, but he carried on.

His third week with the men started with a haircut. One of the men shaved his head clean. At dinner the men complimented him. They told him that personal grooming and hygiene brought a man closer to God and how a man treated himself is how he treats the world. There was a fellowship among the men, or"Gator Boys" as they called themselves, and the Boy was captivated by it. It made him feel a little like the horses made him feel, like he belonged. He didn't understand why, but he didn't care. He only wanted to be part of it.

That evening he found two pair of the alligator boots in front of his hut. He wondered why until he noticed the wax and rag. Putting a shine on shoes was something he was already good at, so he did his best. The boots glowed in the half-light of dawn as the two men collected them. Later that day Ras praised him as they began their walk through the fields."The devil lives in the details, boy. A man gotta be able to see what he gotta do when he gotta do it, all on his own. Ain't nobody gonna hold his hand and lead him through life explaining everything all the time." The Boy smiled to himself and leaned into his work.

Sleepers bothered him. But finding them early was better because they were cold and stiff, easier to carry. Too much time in the sun made carrying them out of the crops difficult because the skin came off the bone like wet paper.

The violence of keeping the rest of the slaves working became an outlet for the Boy. It was a way to forget about the horror. He felt an uncomfortable mixture of shame and betrayal the first time he beat a man. He wasn't defending himself; he was inflicting pain. Ras explained that he was helping the people. "They choose to be here and they need help to follow through with their commitment. You only helping them to keep their word. Helping them to develop the discipline that's gonna see them through the hard days. Everyone needs a little help with this sort of thing from time to time. They the lucky ones. They have this community around them that hold them to certain standards and help them live up to those standards."

The Boy wondered where Ras learned a lot of what he said but he never questioned him. He felt a strong sense of privilege to be near Ras. He also felt something grow inside himself. He couldn't name it but while he listened to Ras he strived to do everything he could to receive acknowledgement.

He also worked hard to push away the memory of being raised by women. He learned quickly to suppress nurturing thoughts and embrace the fierce, hard side of his thinking. It made perfect sense that a little violence was helping those workers work better.

A season of rain came and went. He became good at his new life as a part of the Gator Boys. If he found boots at his door he mended and polished them. If he found an axe he sharpened it. Walking the fields became easier. The dead bodies were unpleasant but infrequent. The near-dead almost always found a way to get to their feet when they heard him coming with his barbed caning stick. His eyes were wide open as he went about his days. He learned to see the things that needed to be done without someone else painfully bringing them to his attention.

He also became good with the bull whip that the men carried. Some of them took time to show him how to use it, how to make it crack the air or bite small chunks out of its target. He learned how to build a fire and stay warm and dry in the wilderness. They chased down small deer and he learned to hunt and butcher them. He could make a shelter and feed himself. He learned how to fight. Twice he was challenged in the crops. His caning stick did him little good and the Gator Boys simply watched. He learned to keep an edge on his knife. He became good at things he'd never dreamt he could do.

That night at dinner Ras asked, "You ready to get yo'self new boots, boy?"

"Yes, Sir!"

"What kinda boots you want?"

Unsure and surprised by the question he blurted out, "Like yours!" By then the men within earshot had quieted until they heard his answer. They exploded with laughter. Ras shouted to the entirety of the men, "The boy wants some Gator in his boots!" And the men exploded again.

The Boy grinned ear to ear. Somewhere deep inside he knew he didn't want to wear boots ever again. But he was elated the men were so happy about his new boots. Like a good soldier he suppressed his doubt and beamed as the men roared and slapped his back and carried on.

Morning broke upon the Boy and Cookie as usual except that Ras and two of the men came riding up hard and fast."-Get on, boy!"

Before he could exhale they were riding at a full run.

He had never ridden so fast. When they finally stopped he swung off the back of the horse and fell, causing the two men to laugh. Ras growled,"Tighten up boy! You wanna be the master of your world? You gonna learn what that looks like today. So you better tighten up!"

The Boy pretended to look stern but was still dizzy. When one of the two men winked at him his smile burst wide once more. They had stopped somewhere he had not seen before. They were still on the plantation but somewhere new. The buildings were small and clean and whitewashed. Very diffe-rent than the low huts that everyone slept in.

Black women were everywhere, dressed in white and as clean as he vaguely remembered from his first home. They reminded him of the white nurses that had tended to master Conner. Today was as hot as any day but the women didn't seem to notice, they didn't sweat. They looked fresh as they shuffled back and forth between the little buildings.

The Boy felt like he was in a dream as he tied the three horses to the rail. Ras stood with his hat in his hands and talked with one of the women in white. The Boy thought of Lily for the first time in a long time. As he moved to join Ras, he noticed the other two men standing at a doorway across the road. They were laughing.

Stepping up to the doorway with the two men he was struck. The smell, pungent, thick, and sweet, he did not recognize. It was opposite the stench of a few days' old sleeper in the crops. Standing at the doorway just behind the men he could taste the smell. It tasted of old sweat and blood. The door had bars on it, like a prison. The room was dark and as his eyes adjusted he began to make out shapes.

A moment later he could see a large man violently undulating onto a woman bent over a small cot on the floor. The man was making an awful grunting and groaning sound, like a dying cow. The woman was staring into the cot and holding on with clenched fists. The Boy was concerned and confused. When the two men noticed him they laughed. He took a step back, unsure of how to feel. That's when he noticed there were a long row of rooms. Bars on the small windows, bars on the doors, the whole building on this side of the street were rooms like this one.

He peeked into three more rooms and saw similar scenes in each. The last one held only a man and he was standing at the iron gate that secured the doorway. He startled the Boy as he reached out to touch him. The man was naked and smelled of alcohol. He had a crazed look in his eyes. The Boy turned and ran to where Ras was still talking to one of the women in white. She turned to leave as he approached, and he sensed she was crying. Ras heard him and barked for him to follow. They walked towards the row of buildings opposite the ones he had ran away from. He exhaled relief as he looked back over his shoulder. The two men were still watching and laughing.

The rooms on this side were bigger and without the jail-like bars. He noticed a few women in each. By the third room he realized they all held babies in their arms. He began to delight inside; he could see the eyes of the women as they nursed their newborn babies. He stopped himself from smiling before Ras noticed. When they got back to the horses the other men had mounted and rode ahead. As he unhitched the horse he noticed the crying woman hand one of the two men a sack and he tied it to his saddle. Ras reached a hand down and the Boy pulled himself up onto the back of the horse.

"Some men are born strong, some made strong, some just lucky I guess. Same for smarts, born, made, whatever. Point being, this world wants to tear you apart. If you ain't strong enough or smart enough you get what the world wants, instead of what you want."

The Boy was only half listening as he still delighted in hearing the babies wailing as they rode out of that place. He didn't understand why he felt the way he did but he also wasn't that interested in figuring it out. He knew the other men would not like it.

A short ride brought the group to a mangrove. The two men set to work building a fire and making camp. The Boy realized that they would be spending the night in the swampy mangrove. He started making a list of chores in his head when he heard the babies crying again. He laughed to himself. He wondered at the power of his own mind, hearing the babies crying when they were nowhere near that strange place. He ran into the thick to find more wood for the fire.

When he returned with an armful of wood the men had cleared a large area in front of the water, about fifty yards from the fire. As he dropped the wood he could see that this clearing had been used for trapping gators for a long time. There was a thick, worn, wooden stake in the middle of the clearing. Ras and the two men were standing at the water's edge looking out across the web tangle of mangroves.

"Get that pig shoulder on the fire and unroll the salted fish so we can eat," Ras said without turning to look at him. He had already begun doing it when he stopped short. He stared and listened and listened harder and stared. He heard babies crying. He knew he heard babies crying but when he turned to look and see if the other men heard the babies crying, they were still looking out over the mangroves. When he turned back around his eyes lighted on the sack that he had seen the crying lady hand over. It was still attached to the saddle but now he noticed that it was moving and crying.

"What the fuck you waiting for, boy?"

He took another step and stopped. He knew the meat was in a similar sack on the other horse, but he couldn't tear his gaze from the moving, kicking sack.

Confused, he pushed forward and retrieved the food stores and opened the cloth that held the dried fish. He unwrapped the pork and found the working spit already near the fire pit. As he assembled the spit he looked back at the sack, it was still and silent. He wondered if he were going crazy. As he forced the meat onto the sharp end of the spit his mind tumbled and fell. The sack erupted. He looked over his shoulder and saw the sack kicking once more and at the same time felt relief and panic. He knew he wasn't crazy but struggled to understand what was happening.

"Don't burn the meat, boy! The Reverend gave us that special so we could stay out here till we find a big one. He wants new boots, boy, how 'bout that? You and the Reverend gonna have boots from the same gator. You should be proud."

He could only hear blood in his ears. His heart was pumping almost out of control, and he backed away from the fire so he wouldn't pass out into it.

"Look like he seen a ghost."

"Nope, He just putting it together. He's sensitive, but we'll cure him soon."

The first drippings of pork fat hit the fire and the flames jumped high into the mid-morning sun. He sat transfixed as the flames dried his tears.

"You let that meat burn and you next, boy!" He kneeled in front of the fire and turned the spit, making sure the fat did not catch fire.

The men unraveled and cut two strands of rope. One man removed the sack from the horse and caused it to kick and scream. He emptied the contents on the beach and secured it to the stake, making jokes about the deformed upper lip and uneven and missing limb. They laughed overly loud and uncomfortable, even for ruthless men.

"Let's eat, boy, this here might take a while. We need to wait for a big one."

"Or two!" exclaimed one of the men followed by more awkward laughter.

The alligators came. They took the bait and died. The men ate and drank, slept and snored. The Boy did not eat, did not sleep, did not speak. They broke camp and saddled up in silence as the sun crawled through the mangroves. They rode home with two fine examples of mature alligators.

CHAPTER 13

The Cobbler

The cobbler's hut was a half mile from the row of huts that house the Gator Boys. The Boy took the horse and cart through the dense jungle. When he emerged into the circular clearing it struck him as another world, or at least one more part of the island he hadn't seen. He wondered how big the island was.

As he approached the group of three huts he looked back at the two large alligators in the cart. He knew they were dead, but you couldn't tell by looking at them. Their dinosaur skin and black eyes had not changed. The endless rows of teeth showing through their gaping mouths remained the same. His stomach squirmed with the thought of the disfigured baby.

"The cobbler and a few helpers make the boots for all us workin' overseers on the plantation, including the Reverend." Ras warned the Boy that the cobbler was a strange man. He said with a laugh, "Makes a mighty fine boot but he don't say much and when he do speak, he sound crazy. Tell him what you need and ignore him if he starts talkin' and you be all right."

When he showed up with the alligators the cobbler seemed uninterested. The Boy stood there holding the reins. Without looking up from his work the cobbler pointed to a stool. The Boy began to utter what he thought the cobbler should know. "These are for a pair of boots for—"

Without looking up, the cobbler held up a hand to signal the Boy to stop talking. Again, he pointed at the empty stool. The Boy sat. The cobbler continued working. Three men approached and began unloading the carcasses. He watched the men wrestle the alligators. Everybody seemed impervious to the big, hard afternoon sun. Not knowing what to do with himself, he closed his eyes and tried to push away thoughts of yesterday. The heat and uncertain silence started the nightmares crawling into his conscious. He fought to keep them at bay when a voice asked, "Are you cut out for this work you've chosen?"

His eyes snapped open, and his jaw stiffened. His heart raced as he tried to make sense of what he thought was a voice in his head. He was a split second away from the horror on the beach when he heard the question again. Startled, he looked around for who was talking to him. The cobbler was still bent to his work. The other men were too far away and unconcerned with him. A second glance found the old cobbler looking into him. The old man's eyes were gray, like they were filled with smoke.

Startled, all he could manage was, "What?"

The cobbler watched him for a moment more and returned to his work.

"I didn't choose this," the Boy finally managed.

«And yet here you are," rose from the old man. "Come back tomorrow and I'll fit you."

He watched the old man a minute more and stood. A confused feeling of regret stirred his guts as he drove the horse and cart back through the jungle.

That night as he stared at the black thatched ceiling from his wood plank cot his mind raced. First the violence. Then wanting to please Ras. *What happens if I disappoint Ras? What would life be like back in the fields? Three men to a hut, never enough to eat. What's in the stew pot?* And back to the violence. Every other round the cobbler's blind eyes would pop into his brain, and his anger grew. *Why would he ask such a question? Why would he think I chose this? What gives that old man the right to even ask? Who does he think he's talking to?*

All these thoughts proved that he might not sleep, again. He began to think about hurting the old man and felt better. The deeper he plotted the more his mind told him he was on the right track. He could tell Ras that the old man had spoken badly of him and his men. Or he could put his knife to the old man, deep enough to scare him. He could sneak over to the cobbler's hut right now and put his knife across his throat and never have to hear the old man again. The Boy slept, with fewer of the usual nightmares.

The sun pushed slits of light over the long horizon and the air began to heat up. The Boy stared at Cookie. The timid cook reminded him of something out of reach and then old Tom flashed through his mind like a ghost. He wondered what became of old Tom. The click and clank of forks on tin plates brought him back to now. As he watched Cookie, he felt a growing disgust for the man. Then he knew what was happening; he had felt the same way about old Tom as he did towards Cookie, but now he knew why. Like Tom the old cook lived on his knees, doing and saying and acting however he was told, afraid of everything and everyone. He also realized that, according to Ras, he chose to live that way. Ras, the Reverend, even Lily, all the powerful people in his life seemed to believe this idea about always having a choice. He felt himself grow beyond disgust and into a hate, he wanted to hurt the old cook. He thought again of hurting the cobbler. As his mind jumped to hurting Ras, he scared himself and jumped to cleaning the abandoned breakfast plates from the long table.

He spent the next hour doing his chores at double speed, hoping to expel the angry thoughts through sweat. When he was walking the fields for sleepers he watched Ras on his horse on the perimeter. He searched Ras and the other men for signs of frustration or doubt. He wondered if they believed they were choosing this life. He felt disconnected from the idea, it confused him; *How could anybody choose this life?* Overseer or slave, it all began to feel terrible to him. The rest of the day he fell deep into a melancholy, longing for how his life used to be. He missed his mother, but as his sorrow twisted into anger, and he corrected himself. *She was my master not my mother.* His whispers turned venomous as he recounted to himself how Lily had forced him to leave the home he loved. He felt a lightness when he recalled putting a shovel to old Tom's face. He wondered if he had killed the old man and whispered aloud, "Better off dead."

The idea calmed him down. His next thought was of the cobbler. The question of choice brought him back to angry. Remembering where he was, he flashed a look up and noticed Ras staring back at him. In the past Ras had reacted with sharp words when asked questions he did not understand or could not answer. The Boy wanted to talk to him about this idea of choice, what it meant, how it worked.

"What's the matter with you, boy?" shouted Ras.

The Boy stopped. He realized he had walked off the field and into the barren one next to it. Standing in the hot sandy dirt and feeling lost, he changed his mind and went mute, responding to the question with a shrug then an apology. Ras seemed unconvinced.

Sitting and sweating in front of the cobbler's hut the Boy plotted. He thought of ways to anger the cobbler. He wondered how he might provoke the old man into violence. He was sure he could beat the old, blind shoemaker. He fingered the blade on his hip as he closed his eyes to the sun and began to doze. He hadn't slept more than a few hours over the past three days.

A warm pulse of electricity shot through him; it was powerful but calming. He was dreaming. He felt a deep comfort, he could feel his feet in a cool, strong embrace. Lily was rubbing the soles with her strong hands as she used to do so often when they were home. As the thumbs pushed deeper into the arches of his feet he felt nostalgic and homesick.

Memories came flickering past his eyes and he realized he had remembered things all wrong. Like shockwaves, the truth came rushing through him. Lily had nurtured his curiosity and encouraged him to learn as much as he could. Lily had taught him how to read. Lily was the one who, gently but firmly explained why he could not tell anyone. Master Conner had tolerated his education. She was the one who finally convinced him to keep it a secret by whipping it into his flesh. Master Conner had taught him to be submissive and dependent. It had been his beloved Lily who was responsible for his secret independence. His unbound curiosity, and idea of possibility buried deep inside his soul was because of her.

The cool, salty tears streaming down his face into the corners of his mouth woke him. The blue-grey, blind eyes looking up at him gave him pause and for a split second he thought he might still be dreaming. Then he realized it was the cobbler kneeling before him and a small fury squeezed his chest. Noticing the old man had his feet in his hands gave that small fury power. He jerked his feet away and stood and took a step back.

"Why would you kill me for asking a question?"

"I'm not going to kill you!" he shouted a little too loud.

"Then why do you have a hand on your blade, boy?"

He looked down at his side and felt surprise mixed with shame as he let go of the worn wood handle."Why are you touching my feet?" Again, a little too loud.

By now the cobbler's helpers were watching."I make boots for those who want them, and I only want to know if you truly want them."

"Why wouldn't I want them?"

"Your feet are young and strong, well callused. You don't need them. I've been a cobbler for a lifetime. I've made boots for kings and soldiers. You are no king. You might one day be a soldier, but for now you are just a boy. So, I simply want to know if you are choosing these boots before I bring them to life."

"I earned these boots!" was all he could manage through his rage and confusion.

"Yesterday you said you did not choose this, have you changed your mind?"

"We killed those gators! Just make the boots, old man, before I change my mind about killing you!"

The cobbler smiled and replied,"You happen to the world, or the world happens to you, that is the first and most important choice we make."

The Boy had to look away knowing he could not follow through with the threat, he knew the old man knew as well. Instead, he shouted at the onlookers."You have a problem?"

He felt even more fake inside, so he doubled down on the threat. He pulled his knife and pointed it at the cobbler"Make the boots!"

CHAPTER 14

The Reverend

The Boy stood on top of the hill in awe. He'd never seen a house so big. He wondered how he hadn't seen it before now. It looked like some mythical castle from a book. The view from the top of the hill was commanding. He could see almost all the plantation that he knew of. This included the tobacco fields, the workers huts, and the overseers' huts to the right. The white-washed row of buildings for the babies and the less-cheerful buildings for the breeding across the street. The only thing you couldn't see was the wagon road that led to the mangroves where the gators were hunted, and the beach itself. The wide blue ocean beyond seemed like a painting. A setting for stories of wild men and wilder beasts, not something for him to understand but an impassable border surrounding his world. At the edge where land met the sea, he squinted to see a row of tiny ships. A procession of tiny horses, carriages, and people moved along the road that led to him.

The six other boys standing with him were the only distraction. He had never seen any of them before. His best guess was that they were from another part of the island. Somewhere he had not been. They dressed exactly like himself, burlap trousers and nothing else. He wondered about the other boys. He wondered about the steady line of carriages and people moving up the lane like an elegant army. The big question was why was he standing on the lawn, in front of the Reverend's house, on top of the island?

After breakfast and the horses, Ras stopped him and told him he needed to go to the Reverend's house. Without explanation he pointed to a path in the jungle and said, "Good luck boy. Do yo' best and you be all right. Give me yo' knife, you'll get it when you get back." He turned his horse and left the Boy standing there wondering.

On his way up the path that switched back and forth as it climbed the steep hill, his mind raced with possibility. He imagined the Reverend congratulating him on the gator hunting, or his ability with the horses. He thought maybe he would hear the teachings that Ras was always going on about, like discipline and duty. He fantasized that the Reverend had recognized his skill and would invite him to work in the house. His heart sped up when he thought he might see Lily. He remembered polishing the silver. He thought of his shoes. He heard the cat and the hammer. His stomach jumped. He remembered betrayal. He breathed deep and carried on.

Lost in the view, he decided he and the other boys were there to help attend to the guests. The fancy procession was obviously a party about to happen. He felt a sense of pride to be part of such a grand party, and to be looking over the land that he was at least a little responsible for overseeing.

He wondered again where the other boys came from as the group spoke in hushed whispers and giggles. His face flashed hot as he stared at the others, he knew the importance of discretion when waiting on the master. A slave should be only occupied with serving. The others seemed to understand only half of the equation. They knew to whisper but they displayed a petty regard for their own lives, lives that meant nothing without the master.

When the Reverend appeared the group of boys turned to stone. They all looked down into the grass as if in prayer. Except the Boy, he regarded the Reverend with wide eyes. He was bursting inside but no-one noticed. The Reverend said nothing. He paused long at the baluster of the porch, looking down at the group. The Boy averted his eyes. The tall thin man spoke. The Boy worried at his own eagerness and wished Ras were here to help him. He finally decided to try and stay calm and do what he was told and do it the best he could like Ras had told him.

The Reverend's voice was gentle. "You boys have come a long way since you got here. You've learned to work; you've learned to follow orders. I hear that each of you have even learned to hunt that most ferocious of beasts the alligator!

You have proven to be a credit to your race, already making this world a better place by learning to follow the white race if only even by a fair imitation. So I welcome you here to help make this land, that the creator has bestowed upon me, great and bountiful. You will do your part today and forever, whether it be blood or muscle you pour into this land. Rejoice, you will entertain our guests today while proving yourselves, but first a surprise."

The Reverend turned and disappeared into the house. A servant, tall and thin and light-skinned enough to pass as white took his place in front of the group of boys.

"Follow me," the servant said with a shovel full of contempt in his voice. The Boy immediately felt that this was where he used to belong. His second feeling was alarm as he followed the house servant. He thought of Cookie. He felt the shovel crack against old Tom's skull. He heard the cat and the hammer. It all felt like a home that was fading from memory, an uncomfortable memory that no longer belonged to him.

The boys marched around the side of the massive house. They followed single file, their bare feet hushed against stone. The click clack of the servant's shoes loud and sharp. As they rounded the back of the house the path opened to a wide pasture. It sloped up for a couple hundred yards. Near the top were the crowds of people that he had watched parade onto the plantation. Behind the crowd were bleachers adorned with red, white, and blue bunting. A dozen red, white, and blue flags snapped in the breeze. When the boys reached the summit they were halted by the servant. They stood opposite the crowd like outnumbered chess pieces a couple hundred yards apart. The boys and the crowd watched the Reverend climb the small, elevated podium. With his back to the boys, he lifted a copper cone-shaped speaking-trumpet to his face and addressed the small sea of silk top hats and white gowns.

The crowd began to notice the boys, they pointed and shouted. The Boy wondered why the Reverend would have them serving his guests shirtless and shoeless. He hoped they would be getting dressed properly, like the servant leading them. Embarrassment filled him so he kept his eyes on the head in front of him and tried to ignore the crowd as the Reverend spoke.

"Ladies and gentlemen, Thank you from the bottom of my heart for joining me here today. I know some of you have traveled a fair distance to be here and again I thank you and hope that your stay here with us is comfortable as well as enlightening.

«As we find ourselves at the middle of this modern century, our burgeoning country faces some difficult challenges. As prosperous as it is, where freedom and opportunity abound, where a man can shape his own destiny as he sees fit, we still have some obstacles to overcome. But with God on our side and old-fashioned ingenuity, I believe we shall!

"I've asked you all here today, as I have every couple of years past, to celebrate a little brotherly communion as masters of this great nation. And also, to share with you some ideas on the challenges we face. I've prayed, pondered, and contemplated on these matters for most of my Christian life. Today I'll not only share solutions with you, but I will also show you the proof of my success so that you may take these ideas and implement them yourselves. So that we can build this great nation strong and everlasting!

«I want to discuss first the issue of the red savage, if only to bring context to the second issue of the black savage. The Godlessness of the Indian makes it so that we, as God-fearing men, must subdue or control these heathens. But circumstances have proven that control is not an option. We are forced instead to eradicate this lower race completely. We will always face opposition from our own misguided countrymen whose bleeding hearts cloud their vision. but I believe that time will prove these actions to be the true and moral course for the prosperity of America.

"The elimination of the red savage comes not from malice of our hearts but from a misplaced attitude of the savage himself. He believes not in the one true God, nor in any semblance of morality. He carries several languages, too many to count in fact, so that there is no unity or common understanding, only a constant tribe against tribe warfare. He insists on cave dwelling or living in the mud. Never cultivating crops but roaming aimlessly and killing and eating like some vile sort of scavenger. It is for these reasons; a fiercely independent attitude, a complete unwillingness to embrace a higher more advanced way of life, and an unwillingness to let us help them, that it is too late for them. This savage species is doomed.

«But it is this second issue that holds the true import of why we are here today. The black savage is redeemable. I have developed systems to enrich the ferocious untamed lives of the African species, to bring them closer to God, and at the same time enrich our economic and social status in the world, in short, to make America great! Most of these tactics are ancient. They've been employed for centuries. I have only refined them here. I think ancient Rome would envy us.

«The first of these I'll share with you today is language. Language speaks to the heart faster than most everything else. It is the most valuable emotional currency, especially with the mud races that do not understand a work of art or a piece of music. To erase the mother tongue and introduce a limited sum of English is to erase a majority of their history. By teaching language limited to the specific life work of the negro; plowing, harvesting, cleaning, it remains a simple thing to communicate our needs and help the savage stay focused while keeping them ignorant and unaware of our means, ways, and goals.

«The second thing we should consider heavily is the breaking of resistance. Like a horse, we will use the same basic principles combined with a few sustaining factors. When we break a horse, we are essentially reducing them from their natural state to a state of dependency. Where nature provides them with the full capacity to take care of themselves and their offspring, we break that natural string of independence from them, thereby creating a dependency status. We are all well aware of the power of a rope and tree, however, the civilized and compassionate nature of a simple hanging creates a need for frequent application. I propose something less civil, more violent, so that we need its employ less and therefore keep this valuable resource alive and working for our benefit. I will go into detail later with those interested and only outline in brief here. The goal being to strip away the natural tendencies and replace those with a complete dependency. At the cost of your biggest, strongest, perhaps meanest, most independent male slave you can set the males, females, and children on a looping path of dependency for the next three hundred years or more. The cycle will turn into itself over and over and only be broken by some extraordinary event.

"Here is the process in short. Gather all your slaves. Take the biggest buck and tie each limb to a horse. Pull him to pieces and burn the pile, while blaming the female he has been breeding. Separate the males from the females. The males will have no choice but to live in submission or die. Force the females to provide for themselves and their children alone, only depending on you, of course. She will in turn teach her male offspring to be submissive from the start. Her female offspring will need not a male figure, or trust in him. Effectively reversing roles and forcing the path to repeat itself well into the twentieth or even twenty-first centuries.

"The third process to consider, and the one that allows me to sleep in complete peace, is distrust. By using the many differences of your chattel; age, sex, color, you can pit old against young, dark skin against light skin, and on and on so that no one savage will trust another and therefore remain separate and powerless. Be assured that distrust is stronger than trust, envy is stronger than respect. You should encourage your overseers, even your spouse and children to reinforce the distrust between slaves at every opportunity. As a bonus you should discreetly assure each slave that they can count on you to take care of them so that they love and trust you alone.

"A quick word on breeding. It is necessary to introduce a few drops of pure white blood into as many female slaves as possible from time to time. This helps create the differing skin tones to separate them as well as keep the stock strong.

"We will go further into all of this business over the next couple of days I'm sure, but let's not forget to enjoy ourselves also! I have a grand spectacle planned for you next! A play of sorts. An exhibition of the black beast in its natural condition! It's sure to get your blood pumping and give you a rapacious appetite, of which you will need for the feast I have prepared!"

The Boy listened to the speech as the other boys either gawked at the crowd or stared at the ground. The Reverend's talk of duty made him stand a little taller. He thought of Ras and understood where he'd learned his philosophy on responsibility. The easy talk of violence made him cringe as he realized that he had become more like a beast. Killing the cook's helper for no good reason was barbaric. He felt violence for the sake of violence inhumane, but it was part of becoming a man. His pulse quickened as he thought back on his selfishness and ignorance as a young servant for the Conners' and marveled at how much he had grown. He compared that to his new self, his strength, self-reliance, his freedom to make choices for himself. A smile grew as he realized that he was the only one in his group that understood most of what the Reverend was preaching. He glanced at the elegantly dressed servant staring at the ground and felt superior. He felt certain that after today the Reverend would look at him as the best of the bunch. Together with Ras, they would run the place better than ever.

An audible whoop erupted. He noticed the Gator Boys riding up towards the top of the berm. His excitement was electric. He imagined what might be next; showing off his riding skills alongside Ras or working together as a group to show how effective they all were. His mind reeled with possibility. When the riders got close he studied Ras's face, looking for the shared admiration they usually expressed. Ras's face was hard and cold. All the riders wore a battle face. He knew it was part of the show and assumed a similar persona, looking straight ahead and standing strong and tall.

The riders stopped behind the row of boys, close enough that he could feel the hot breath of the horses on his neck.

He had never felt prouder as he realized he was a part of something special, a brotherhood, or a small battalion of soldiers, like Sparta. He felt safe.

The Reverend spoke."This is proof that the methods I have laid out for you today do in fact work. These riders are shining examples of a primitive savage exercising freedom of choice. Loyal to God, loyal to me, and loyal to themselves. Choosing to govern their beastly nature and encouraging others of their race to do the same." The Reverend turned towards the riders and waved a hand.

When the whips began to crack everything changed. He looked over his shoulder, asking Ras what to do. His response was a biting snap of leather to his cheek from his mentor.

Half the boys received the whip as the other half moved forward to avoid the stinging snap. The riders were driving the boys forward too fast for him to make sense of it all. As they crested the small berm the whipping ceased, and the boys stood gazing at something they struggled to understand. A table set with extravagant food, roasted meat, baked bread, and sweets. Beyond the table it became more of a grassy depression that you could only see if you were standing around its edges. From the top it was a sloping six feet to the bottom and fifty feet across. The round pit had been unnoticeable from where the boys stood. The ground sloped up and away on all sides. Wooden bleachers filled with the Reverend's guests looked down on everything. Parasols and top hats jumbled together atop a hundred voices suddenly filled with merriment. The sun shone down silent and heavy on the entire spectacle.

None of the boys moved a muscle. They stood and stared first at the crowd, then at each other, then at the table, and again at the crowd. Still unsure of what to do, they continued the triangle of looks, the table, the crowd and each other. It seemed like the entirety of the guests had assembled up there by now. The Boy's brow furrowed in dread as he tried to understand what was happening. The crowd stirred. "Eat! Eat! Eat!" they began to chant.

He had never felt so alone. He heard the shotgun blast from the den, the shovel breaking Tom's face, the hammer and the cat, as blood rushed to his ears, drowning out the crowd. In another moment most of the boys in unison approached the table and sat down, eyes wide and lips smacking. He and another boy noticed that they were standing there alone, exposed. They sat with the others as the crowd roared "Eat! Eat! Eat!" The boys began to eat. After a minute or two they were in full-blown frenzy, except for him and one other boy. He wanted to cry. He and the other boy put some food on their plate in compliance. His stomach was so twisted and tangled that he could barely look at the food let alone eat any. He sat, and watched, while the others gorged.

Out of the corner of his eye he noticed a servant approaching the table. It was a female, and she carried a large crock. As she poured something into each boy's cup the smell of rich fruit filled his nostrils and turned his stomach.

"Eat! Eat! Eat!" The chant continued but his hearing started to muffle again. The chanting seemed far away. The gnawing and slurping of teeth and his own heartbeat drowned everything. He could feel the heat in his face. He thought he might pass out as he grabbed hold of the table and held on.

After a half hour the boys at the table had all stopped eating. The laughing and cheering of the crowd seemed only concerned with itself. Two boys lay on the ground grinning and moaning and rubbing their swollen bellies. They talked about how they felt dizzy. One boy slept where he sat, his head on the table, his cup of wine spilled out in front of him, food still in his mouth. The Boy still had a grip on the table. The muted sounds and tunnel vision started to relent. He looked to the other end of the table and studied the passed-out boy. He watched him choke on the food half spilling out of his mouth then he came awake and spat hard. Food sprayed out in front of him. He put his head back down. In a flash he was back in his barn at home watching old Tom snore into a pile of hay still clutching an empty bottle. He knew the boys were drunk; he had heard Lily explain old Tom's behavior with disgust.

In front of him was a full cup of wine, the smell reminding him of an apple orchard gone rotten. Sitting up straight and leaning back so he couldn't smell the wine, he took a deep breath in. As he exhaled he looked around, trying to make sense of what was happening.

"They're going to make us fight." The voice came from nowhere. He half turned to the boy who spoke.

"What?"

The strange boy was silent.

"But why?"

The boy looked him in the eyes but said nothing. After a long moment the Boy put his focus back on the two boys rolling around on their backs laughing at each other.

"You heard the man. It's a show, we're the show." The strange boy seemed to be talking to himself.

"You don't know what you're talking about," he replied. He had heard the speech. He knew the boy was right, but he did not want to believe it.

He flashed back to the cook's helper, the men cheering and betting, the wine, the knife, the blood. He thought of his knife and remembered that Ras had taken it from him. He heard drums and wondered if he were starting to pass out again. He didn't remember any drums when he'd killed the cook's helper. The sharp crack of a bullwhip brought him back to now. Three of the Gator Boys on horseback were stomping around the table shouting orders and hitting the boys with whips. All the boys were on their feet, even the sleeping boy. The men on horseback drove the boys down into the large grass pit. They stood, staring wide-eyed at each other.

The crowd began to roar so loud that he could feel it through his body. His heart burst from his chest in direct competition with the crowd. The others standing next to him were in different states of awe, some smiling, others wide-eyed and confused. One throwing up everything he had just devoured. He noticed the one who had been passed out at the table start to dance to the drums. He could feel the drums sound more than hear them. He felt like he was going deaf: the sounds, the jagged drums, and the roar of the crowd seemed to be coming from miles away. As his hearing diminished his vision started to tunnel. Everything slowed down, time struggled to move. He began noticing tiny details of the scene.

The drums were tall native looking drums carved from wood. The players were three white men with their skin painted black wearing cloth around their waists and shirtless. The rhythm was ugly and uneven. Individuals in the crowd were screaming. Most seemed angry. Some were smiling but all their faces were bright red, and their clenched fists punched the air. One face in the crowd, a woman, was crying. The small umbrella she held somehow highlighted the tears on her cheeks and she was staring straight into his eyes. He thought of master Conner. The panic of the moment made space for a deep yearning in his stomach as he remembered home.

One of the men cut away the burlap trousers of each of the young men and shoved them forward. He only realized this as he was being shoved out of his memory. The crowd in its entirety began to chant, "Fight! Fight! Fight! Fight!"

The Boy stood naked and afraid. His eardrums ached. He covered his ears with his hands and anger crept in to murder the fear. Fury spread like fire. It spread from the crowd to the other young men, to Ras for not protecting him from this, or at least warning him. Rage filled him, but it was the cobbler's words that burned hot: "Is this what you choose?"

The question, or more importantly the answer was what boiled his blood. The first blow from one of the boys connected, he sensed it more than felt it. He was struck in the face again before he was able to get out of his head and into the fight.

It was the biggest of the group, the one that had been asleep at the table. He was drawing back to strike again but he was slow, and his first two blows were glancing. The Boy struck back hard and fast, the big boy dropped like a tree, face first.

Somehow, he stood outside of the chaos that was the others tangled in a mass of blood, sweat, fists, and kicks. The crowd still roared but the grunts and powerful breathing were the only thing he could hear. Two boys wrestled off the heap. Two more laid heavy blows to the boy on the bottom until turning on each other. The boy on the bottom moved awkwardly for a moment then stretched out rigid and stopper moving. The last two boys standing locked their heaving, spitting, bloody attention on him and charged. The veneer of blood and sweat had made the grass too slick to move fast. He could no longer hear the crowd and for a second wondered if they had taken offense at the brutality. He watched the two bodies coming at him in slow-motion. He lashed out with rage.

He came to on his back, choking. He sat halfway up to spit out blood and then a tooth. His ribs cut into him. He looked up as the last boy standing kicked him square in the chest. As he struggled to take a breath he began to vomit. He was choking and gasping, trying with everything he had to sneak a breath between heaves of bile. His vision began to blur as he watched the big boy he had put down a moment ago walk up behind the boy that had kicked him and put a headlock on him. The big boy's nose was crushed to his face. Blood ran free, staining his gritted teeth pink. He breathed so hard in and out that spit and blood sprayed like a light rain.

He began to black out as the big boy lifted the other boy off the ground and screamed like a wounded animal. The noise shocked him awake. He watched the boy in the headlock claw at the powerful arms around his neck. His eyes bulged from his face with terror. The dull crack ripped through the air and the hanging boy shit himself. The big boy screamed even louder. The crowd thundered again but he could only hear the big boy scream. He heaved and choked and spat. His throat burned. He struggled to breath. His ribs cut into him with every breath. His tongue found a hole in his cheek.

The big boy wailed but did not let go of the dead, broken boy. He hung like a doll, wiggling to the rhythm of the big boy's wailing. At his feet lay a boy face down, he was not breathing. Another boy was moaning. He watched the big boy holding the other boy off the ground. He dropped the dead boy. There was a horse standing over him and he did his best to curl into nothing so the horse didn't step on him. He sensed the horse hesitate, his big black eye looking down at him with concern. The Gator boys were herding the big boy out of the putrid heap of bodies, blood. They were shouting congratulations at the big boy.

"Good job, boy!" And to each other, "Had my money on the big gorilla the whole time!" Once they had him standing apart, they rode back up the hill. The big boy stood and stared at the crowd. He breathed softer now, but blood mixed with slobber still dripped from his face.

The Boy lay on his back trying to control his breathing and through closed eyes he could hear a man talking. He couldn't make out what the man was saying. He struggled to stay conscious and began to let himself slip away. As he began to fall into sleep he made out a few words from the man speaking, "Winner… Too fast… Prize… Watch him breed…!" He was awake long enough to see a girl tied at the neck, being led behind a horse. She was young, wearing only terror. He did not stay conscious long enough to see the big boy grin wide, showing his pink bloodstained teeth, and take the girl right there in the defiled grass. The crowd roared anew.

He woke up in his rope cot. He wondered how long he'd slept. He couldn't open his eyes. He gently touched the dried blood that crusted them shut. The right side of his face was swollen so thick it felt like the skin might rip open. As he began to roll on his side to get out of bed lightning stabbed his lungs and a hammer began ringing his head. He lay flat and still. By the smell and heat he could tell it was late in the day. He listened. He narrowed the time by the movement of the outside world that he could hear above the ringing. He put together pictures of what was happening outside his little hut. Wood was being split for the iron pot that fed the men. No voices, so the men were still overseeing the fields. No birds sang during the height of the day. Under the quiet, even deeper under the ringing, he could hear nails tapping into wood.

The cobbler's words rose above the hammer in his head."You happen to the world or the world happens to you. Because freedom is freedom, never something like freedom and it starts inside a man."

Yesterday had convinced him that the old blind slave was right. He could see that he had chosen to fight. If he had chosen not to fight and remained passive he might be dead. The sound of a neck breaking and the squeal of the big boy marshaling all his strength slipped in before he could slam the door of his mind shut. The smell of shit and blood followed. Tears burned his swollen eyes and face. He realized that he believed he had no choice. That his destiny was in the hands of the master of this plantation. He believed he was a slave. Even Ras had more control over his life than he did because Ras believed something different. Ras believed he had choices, true or not. He remembered the fear in the cook's helper's eyes and Ras's certainty. Thinking back to the beach, where he first laid eyes on Ras, again his own fear and Ras's certainty.

Going back further, to his beloved house, he realized he was trading fear for duty, obedience for food and shelter. He had repressed all his own wants and feelings to stay out from under the whip. He hated old Tom and the cook because he could see his own fear in them.

He lay broken and bruised, unable to move under an ocean of emotion. Then Lily flashed into view. He saw her as if she walked through the wall. He could see her reading to him like he was standing in the corner of the room. He heard her whispering in his ear with grave sincerity to "Never let anyone know." He watched her tie his shoes. He listened to her explain how to serve dinner to guests and remain unseen while doing it. He traveled back to before he was able to remember, Lily telling him stories of when she was a child, a free child. He understood that it was Lily, not master Conner who had taught him everything.

Like a snake bite, the painful truth seeped into him. The false memories burned in his veins. Why had he remembered it wrong? Why did he want to take that from her? Lily had given him all of her, and he gave her contempt in return. He had abandoned the only gift this hard world had given him. His broken bones felt hollow in comparison.

"Come out here, boy!" Ras shouted.

The Boy stirred from his reverie. He dreaded leaving his new recollections of himself and his past. He did not want to face the present. He knew that outside the door to his little hut was a future he did not choose. He was beginning to understand how easy it was to fool himself, to choose a story over the truth. His mind raced. He knew a few things in his heart. He would not continue to be the man that Ras wanted any longer than it would take, and he was leaving this place with Lily if he could find her. The future was his to decide.

The Boy spent another full day and night in bed before Ras and some of the men rousted him up and out for good. They forced him into a tub of water with a chunk of perfumed soap and they laughed. The men laughed at his swollen face. They laughed when he couldn't chew his food. They laughed when he yelped with pain. They made jokes about the stench. They even joked about two of the seven boys not living through the weekend's entertainment. They called it entertainment, that convinced him these men were animals dressed in pants and shirts.

He thought back to how certain he had been that physical strength and fast, violent hands were something to be proud of. He tried to suppress the bile rising in his throat. It wasn't the dead that sickened him. It was the living, the men making jokes. The spectators in that crowd. All of them, even the woman who saw him, the woman who cried for the brutality of it all. He wondered how Christians could thirst for blood. He thought he understood why his kind seemed immune to violence, being closer to animals than to men. But the white race had the Bible, straight from the mouth of God. They had commandments. They built temples to God. The Boy yearned for an explanation.

CHAPTER 15

The Cobbler

Sitting with the cobbler felt comforting and treasonous at the same time. As if the Boy were turning on himself somehow. He instinctively believed the cobbler would show him things that contradicted what he thought he knew. Things he'd been taught by the only man that ever cared for him might be wrong and that worried him.

"Are you going to answer me or not?"

"You already know, boy, or you wouldn't be so upset."

"But I don't know! I have no idea how you can read the Bible, have God in your heart, and enjoy someone being torn apart. All at the same time! Please just tell me!" His blood-shot eyes pleaded with the cobbler's smoke-smeared eyes.

The cobbler sat on his haunches and worked the rough hide with a heavy needle and sinew. "So much untruth has been taught for so long that it seems impossible that it is not true. But if you can open your mind and hear what I say you might have a chance to understand.

"In the beginning of this world only God was here, and God does not write books. God is the creator of this world, of man and beast. So all men are connected, but different by degrees. For instance, you are a man. I am a man. Despite the shade of your skin or the color of your eyes, we are obviously men. Men and beasts are also connected. We both make plans, however simple. But unlike beasts, men live unsatisfied. A cow eats grass, it will never wonder into the tobacco to feed. We, on the other hand, always want for something more, it is our nature. Whether we strive for more is up to the individual, but the constant want is always there. The only difference among us is what we strive for and why. Some men want comfort. Some men want gold. Some men want everything, and some men want to hide from it all."

The Boy shifted in his seat.

"You know this much, in your heart at least. It is why a man wants what he wants that is of the most importance. A man's inspiration is the key to who he is. This word 'inspiration' is from 'inspire,' which means God's breath within us. Smarter men then I have twisted the truth. The preacher teaches that God is apart from us. This separateness of God allows us to believe that we are separate from each other. We are free of accountability. We are free to sin and be forgiven, free to search outside of ourselves to find meaning. This is the great untruth that man has embraced."

"But why is that important as long as you find God?"

"Because a man searching for meaning outside himself can be easily led astray. All the answers you will ever need are within you. A man searching outside himself for God is like a wave searching for the ocean. He will be lost in the very midst of what he is searching for. So lost that he will listen to anyone that speaks with authority."

"But how is a child supposed to know who he is?"

"If you look to me to tell you who you are and I tell you that you are an animal, if I treat you like an animal, what will you believe, how will you act, what will you strive to be? This is why the first few years of life are so important. We all need a guide in the beginning. Without this we are lost for certain. Look around and tell me if you see this in practice and on purpose. As a man, only you can know who you are. Only you can know for certain what you want."

"How?"

"First decide what you want. Think hard about why you want that thing or feeling or whatever that may be. Then you will begin to understand who you are. And this process never ends, a man must grind through this over and over. Sometimes you will find beauty, sometimes you will find darkness. A man must adjust and keep moving forward, always considering who he wants to be and why. This is the way to be one with God. This is what God intends."

"Why are there masters and slaves?"

"It is simple to do what you are told, and most of us prefer simple."

"That only explains the slave."

"Slaves create masters. If you look for meaning outside of yourself you are sure to find someone that will give it to you. Even a perceived master might simply be pursuing the wants and needs of his father, or other men around him. Do you call him master or just another man with power? We can be slaves in the field breaking our backs. We can be slaves on horses breaking the backs of others. We can be slaves standing on a grand porch, beholden to everything in front of us."

"Because he might not want all that?"

"His reasons why he wants it is the difference between master and slave. A lot of men want what their community wants."

"Why?"

"You know very well the answer. Why do you terrorize others with your cane and whip? If you can be honest with yourself, you will be moving closer to knowing yourself, moving closer to knowing God."

CHAPTER 16

Before Freedom

The chair was tall. He couldn't recall ever seeing it, but he liked it. He also liked that they were on the beach. Ras had cut his hair before but never on the beach. He sat back into the chair and closed his eyes as Ras's strong hands separated his hair with a comb. The tug and pull on his scalp was a mixture of pain and pleasure. He liked the attention. The sun warmed his half smile, and the salt air filled his nostrils. "I got you boy." Ras reassured. "I'ma keep yo' head right, always."

The gentle surf and chatter of seabirds lulled him into a half sleep. Ras finished with the razor and applied the cool stringent tonic to his clean scalp. The Boy wondered if this is what having a father felt like. He sensed a belonging so strong he thought he might be dreaming when Ras began to chuckle. He wanted to ask what was so funny, but he couldn't say the words.

He opened his eyes. The beach was pure white, like light. He knew there were parts of the island he hadn't seen yet; this must be one of them he reckoned. He started to question Ras, but Ras spoke first.

"Fool."

Unsure, he tried to turn and look at Ras, but strong hands forced his face forward.

A hundred yards down the beach a woman walked toward them. He squinted through the burning sun and bright white sand. A woman in a black dress stumbled through the sand, carrying something on her head. He smiled, still feeling the hands firm on his face. He wanted to ask Ras what she was doing but he just kept looking. In a moment he noticed it was a big book she carried on her head. As he noticed the book, the lady noticed them and began walking toward them. He tried to laugh but couldn't. Smiling was the best he could do; he couldn't make a sound. He hoped Ras could tell with his hands that he was smiling. The Boy repeated *fool* in his head.

The lady stopped and stood in the hot sand. With both hands she balanced the large book on her head. She let go the book with one hand and pointed at the Boy. The thin arm extended into a shaky finger that stole his breath. It was Lily.

Seconds turned to hours as he struggled to breathe. His heart raced and his hands groped at the hands holding him. He couldn't scream. He tried. Lily pulled the pointed finger back and looked at her hand. She wailed like a wounded animal, then she stopped and smiled looking deep into his eyes. With obvious struggle she lifted the book off her head and brought it to her bosom. She clutched the heavy book and turned and walked toward the water.

He strained to get out of the chair, to scream Lily's name. Ras had him in a headlock now as he kicked like a wild animal. Sand flew but he could not break free or make a sound. Ras squeezed tight with the strength of a man in combat. The Boy's entire body danced apart from his head as he watched Lily walk into the glittering surf. Lily was waist deep, embracing the book when he felt Ras digging his fingers into his forehead. Blood trickled into his eye as Ras opened a hole in his skull.

"I gotta get this out." Ras whispered through gritted teeth. One eye filled with blood, the other filled with sweat. He watched a blurry Lily sink beneath the waves. He fought and screamed in silence. Ras suddenly released him, having got what he was digging for. The Boy jumped to his feet. The seabirds were silent. His vision was crisp and clear. The ocean sparkled like a million diamonds as far as he could see. He screamed"No!" and woke himself from the nightmare. He tried to catch his breath. He clutched the ground beneath him soaked with sweat. The inside of his hut was dark. The night outside was quiet.

He would save her. He would take her away from this place. He would find Lily and they would escape. Even if it was
her fault they were here, he would make it right. He didn't
know where they would go but he would save her.

He resolved to pay better attention to everything around
him. He would take his time. He would ask gentle questions.
He would watch. He would do this right, for Lily. He remembered his first few moments on the island, on the beach. The
Reverend had given a speech. He had said that anyone was
free to leave. What he meant, it occurred to him only now,
was that anyone was free to choose to stay and serve or choose the ocean and its vast uncertainty. He needed a plan. He
knew he was on an island. He knew he and Lily had to leave
the island. He began to understand that a boat was the only
way out. He had to choose the ocean. He refused to consider
where that boat might take them, but it was the boat that
would set them free.

As dawn crept in, he readied the horses. He remembered
the gator hunt, the beach, the row of small skiffs tied to the
mangroves with meager rope. The boats were small but deep
and big enough for three or four people. Could he fill one
with enough food and water he thought. How much food
and water would they need. How long would they be in the
boat. He thought back to the only other time he'd been on a
boat, that was two nights. So maybe they only needed two
days' worth of food and water. He knew he could go two days

without, but could Lily? And would they go back to where they'd come from? Would he even know how to get back there? There must be a better place to go.

"The territories!" he spoke out loud to the horses, as they all stopped to listen. He smiled to himself and explained to the horses about the wild places in his books. Walking towards the cook fire in the cool dawn he steeled himself. He felt more committed to saving Lily than anything in his life. He needed the cobbler.

That night the moon was bright and he moved fast. It took him thirty minutes at a moderate run to get to Gator Beach. It felt like a race. He wondered how fast Lily could move.

The three boats sat in a row, their bows pointed up, beckoning to him like happy beggars with their hands out. He smiled and knew he would be successful. In the moonlight he could see that only rotten moldy ropes held them to the mangroves. This will be easy, he thought as he approached. He studied the boats and wondered what he should be looking at or looking for.

Looking into the hulls of the three matching skiffs stopped his breath. They were full of water. He took a step back and tried to make it okay in his mind. "Rainwater," he whispered out loud. Looking closer he noticed the three hulls were sinking into the mud. He breathed faster. The moldy ropes arched from the bows to the stunted trees and mocked him with a half-smile.

A slow panic squeezed his chest as he began to hear the crowd chant"Fight! Fight! Fight!" He breathed deep, listening to the chant. He decided to fight.

He climbed in the first boat and baled water with his hands. He worked at this until he was only ankle deep. He felt the bottom of the hull with his hands, tracing the contour above and below the water still inside. He wasn't sure what he was doing but it was the only thing he could think to do, the only way he could fight. The wood felt firm. He found no holes. Maybe it really was rainwater.

He moved to the second boat, and the third. He emptied them of water the best he could. He worked in something like a trance, not counting time, not feeling the fatigue. Standing back on the beach surveying the trio of skiffs he felt the sun trying to crack the sky. There would be more work, but it would have to wait for another day. He thought back to standing in the river, when he made the choice to stay with the Gator Boys and do the violent work of an overseer. He smiled and ran back thinking about the future. Imagining the life he wanted.

Dawn broke on him bent to his work at the cook pot. He hadn't slept and was ahead of his usual chores for the day. He planned on seeing the cobbler after he walked the fields. He was stuck on how to get one of the boats out of the mud. He knew he could repair the small boat if given the chance. If he could only get it up out of the mud to assess the damage, to make a plan. It was only eight feet long and a few feet wide, but too heavy to lift by himself.

It was small but plenty big enough for Lily and himself. All he needed was some water, biscuits, and a hook and line to catch a fish with. He was sure that's all he would need to get somewhere else, anywhere else. He would be sure to ask the cobbler about supplies too.

The sharp crack of bone on bone interrupted his daydream. He found himself on his back, looking up into the breaking daylight. All he could see was an enormous shadow standing over him. Men laughed just behind the shadow.

"See you finally back to work!" He recognized the voice as the sting of the kick exploded throughout his entire face. "I'll have me some food when you done layin' on yo' back!"

The laughter came again but this time it competed with the ringing in his head. He put the voice to a face and realized it was the hulking boy who had won the fight a week ago. His next thought was that it seemed like months since the fight. Then anger, not at the boy but at his situation, he seemed helpless to do anything. Why would this boy attack him?

Instead of charging him with his knife and opening his stomach, he rose and filled the big boy's waiting bowl. The men laughed. The boy smiled and started to speak until the glint hit his eye from the knife returning to its concealment. The big boy froze for an instant then moved on with his breakfast and status intact.

Ras had explained that the fight was to weed out the weak ones, and to see who could handle the job. Ras also shared that he was still okay because he put up a good fight.

"What about the others?"

Ras replied, "What about 'em?"

After breakfast the cook came close and whispered, "I tried to tell you but you was woolgatherin.'" He ignored the cook. He realized the attitude of some of the men had changed since the fight. He was desperate to talk to the cobbler.

He walked the fields without looking at Ras. He did not find any sleepers. After brushing down the horses he rushed to the cobbler's shack.

"They treat you different now," the cobbler spoke to his work in front of him. "You don't understand why," he added as he seemed to look deep into the wood and leather sole of his work.

"I know why. I lost the fight."

"If you only see what is in front of you, you will never see the truth."

The Boy smiled for the first time in forever, he found it funny when the blind cobbler talked about seeing things.

"Most men, weak or strong, smart or not smart, respect responsibility. Your job involves a good deal of violence, it is inherent in the control of men."

"I can do the job! Better than some of the others!"

"But your heart is not in it. We can all see that. Those men see your attitude as disrespectful, as spoiled. This will make them angry, or spiteful, either way it is dangerous for you."

He looked into his open hands and knew the cobbler was right. He also felt the cobbler was warning him, saying something unsaid.

"What happened to your smile?"

He snapped his gaze to the blind man staring back at him, but before he could answer the cobbler spoke. "It is not you alone who is being judged by your attitude."

He knew the cobbler was talking about Ras. "Ras can take care of himself. His heart is in it. He's a monster of a man."

"Some men cannot afford to wear their heart on the outside."

Confused, he changed the subject. "How do I fix the boat?"

After a long, dead silence he began to think he had reached beyond the cobbler's knowledge.

"Fixing the boat is easy. Surviving the sea will be the difficult part."

The Boy sneered. All the interactions with the cobbler came rushing back to him. He felt the cobbler was right, but he didn't know how or why. The boat seemed to be the most important part of his plan; he could not understand any different.

"I have made the three legs three times since I was your age."

"What does that mean?"

"Ships leave Europe with guns and steel. They make their way to the African continent where they trade those things for people, like you and me. Then they sail here to trade you and me for the things that we produce: tobacco, coffee, sugar. They sail back to Europe with these commodities and the process starts over again."

"I've never been on a ship."

"For a long time now America has outlawed bringing us from the continent. Slavers find their way around that easy enough, but also, America has learned to breed her slaves. Right here on this island the Reverend has been perfecting the process, and we've been helping him."

The Boy wanted to disagree but sat quiet.

"Perhaps you should embrace this life you have here, it may be too much risk for you to leave this place."

"I need a boat. I mean, I need to fix a boat."

"The boat is the easy part. The ocean is what you should be concerned about. Who do you know that has made a trip over the ocean, besides me, of course?"

Ras. He saw it like a bright light.

"Be cautious with your inquiries, perhaps be flattering and you may learn quite a bit. But be quick, time is our only true master."

"Why can't you tell me what I need to know?"

"We must all abide time and mine is short for this place."

He frowned and wondered if the old man were becoming senile.

The cobbler stood. "It is difficult to believe what you cannot see. I understand your doubt. But I have faith in you." He placed the alligator boots in the Boy's hands. They shone bright in the afternoon sun. The polish made the leather and skin seem wet. The Boy could see deep into them, *like looking into water* he thought.

"To help you go, or help you stay. Either way, farewell."

The old man turned toward his shack. The Boy looked into the boot leather. He watched the cobbler's reflection disappear into the shine on the boots.

That was the last time he saw the cobbler. He returned two days later, and every trace of the blind man was gone. The three small huts were there but no helpers, no hides, no tools.

He thought the old man must have died. He stood and stared for a moment, mourning his lost friend. He whispered into the evening air, "I will be free. I will find Lily and leave this place." He kicked the dirt with his new, uncomfortable boots as he turned and ran to dinner.

His duties became effortless. The horses were still a joy. Dealing with the cook fire, the pots, and the Gator boys became little puzzles to complete. The dead bodies in the field were lighter. The beating of the living bodies in the field became vital to his mission; to gain the men's trust.

"Dey can't work if you kill 'em!" Ras shouted across the high tobacco.

He looked up from his work with the caning stick and smiled. "Then I'll kill 'em some more!"

As his boots became a little softer and more bearable, the persona of the group began to show through him. He began to walk taller with his chest a little bigger. He challenged men that he knew he could. He made jokes about the violence. He made a point to ridicule the big boy. They warmed to each other. He noticed Ras smiling more.

Over the next few months things changed. "Tomorrow mornin' you get dem horses ready and come eat breakfast. Ain't no more cookin' for you, boy."

In the morning when he arrived at the cook fire, he found a young boy feeding it. The boy was half dressed in rags and had a swollen left eye. He watched him and felt superior. When he heard Cookie grunting instructions it took him right back to his first day. His prideful feelings evaporated into the cool morning air. The boy couldn't be more than eight years old. He looked up from his work and sneered.

At breakfast Ras mentioned they would be going out to hunt gator soon.

"You okay, boy?"

"I'm just surprised. Who needs boots?" He thought fast about the midnight work he'd been doing on the boats and prayed that no one would notice.

"What you care? That ain't none our business."

He smiled at Ras. Ras smiled"You might see yo' mama dis time."

The boy could feel the entire table watching him in a hush, waiting. Blood filled his face.

"More likely to see yo' mama," He replied as flippantly as he could manage. The table exploded in laughter, including Ras. The Boy smiled to himself, trying to slow the storm inside. *Was Ras talking about Lily? Was she alive? Was she at the baby farm?*

"Yo' mama gonna love what I got!" He blurted out and the table erupted again. He didn't know exactly what it meant.

He was repeating things he had heard. He had been trying hard lately to talk like the men, trying harder to fit in. It was working.

The next morning they rode towards the baby farm. The Boy, on his own horse, rode next to Ras. "Lily ain't my mama."

"I know, boy. I was jus' playin' wit' ya."

"She work at the baby farm?"

"She do. I figured you might want to see her. It's okay. I understand. Besides, you earned it."

"Whatever, I don't care." He held his breath until Ras seemed to believe the lie, then he quickly changed the subject. "Why not use a goat or somethin' instead of a baby to catch the gators?"

"Dem littles ain't right. They ain't no good cause they can't work."

The Boy stayed quiet, listening to the horses.

"Besides, goats is meat and milk. We lucky to have 'em."

The sky shined bright as they rode into the farm. Women bustled and the Boy could hear babies crying. He scanned the faces with a hidden fury.

"She in that first buildin'," Ras said pointing with his chin. The Boy followed his nod and right there, through the open window, sat Lily. She was dressed in all white, a bonnet covering her head. He recognized her instantly. She held a bundle in her arms and sat rocking in a chair. Her eyes were closed and an unfamiliar calm shaped her face. His horse kept moving and he kept staring. He tried to break his gaze but he felt paralyzed. He hadn't seen her in over three years. He felt a lump rising in his chest.

She flashed open her eyes and looked directly at him. She seemed to say that she knew what he was doing there. She knew he had turned into a violent thug, that he deserved to be a slave, that he deserved the alligator boots.

He yanked at the reins, turning his horse towards the other side of the road. He rode towards the simple rectangle structure with the bars on the windows and doors. He tied his horse to the post and joined the other two men at one of the barred doors. They were ogling the action inside the room. It looked like a fight to the Boy, like violence. He kept watching simply to avoid looking over his shoulder and seeing her see him. The pair inside the room got louder and the men watching got quiet. The Boy felt something growing inside of him and felt shame. Confused, he peeked over his shoulder and saw her. Her eyes remained closed. She had not moved. She did not see him. He walked back to his horse and away from the grunting shame.

"Where you goin', boy? Dis how dey make 'em. You gonna hafta learn pretty soon!" The men laughed.

He caught up with Ras, who already had the sack tied to his saddle. It was still, but the Boy could see it kicking. It was silent but he could hear it screaming.

He could hear the cat and the hammer. As he trotted ahead of Ras toward the beach he focused on the future. He plotted to save Lily.

The baiting and killing of the alligator went unnoticed. He prepared the chain and hook. He built the fire and put dinner on the spit, but his attention was on the boats, without looking at them. This proved too difficult, so he became distracted with daydreams of saving Lily, of escape.

It wasn't until they tried to load the beast onto the cart that he realized the men were more excited than usual. He realized they had been loud about the gator for a while as he stepped back and became aware of how big it was. At over twelve hundred pounds and almost twenty-two feet long the four of them struggled to lift it. The men spent some time talking about how to transport it without ruining the hide. They decided to build a travois and pull it with two of the horses. He followed orders and after an hour they abandoned the idea.

He stood marveling at the beast. In the background he heard, "We'll take this boat apart and use it like a travois." He unconsciously sprang into action, saying more than he had in twenty-four hours.

"We should take this one. It's half rotted out and will weigh less. It's gonna take all four horses to pull this thing so we should take this one."

The three men watched him, unsure of what was happening.

"We'll break off the transom and benches so we can pull him up into the boat easier."

He began tearing off the back of the rottenest boat with his hatchet. Fear turned to relief as he realized how bad the rot was. It wouldn't have lasted an hour in the water. Minutes later they were tying up the gator to pull him into the hollow hull of the boat when one of the men asked, "How you know so much about boats?"

He froze. "What?"

"Transom. How you know that?"

Not wanting to mention the cobbler he stuttered. His face flushed hot.

"Ras taught me years ago, on the way here!" He shouted too loud. Ras smiled.

On the way back the sun was hard on their faces. He felt like a victorious soldier returning from battle. Not because of the gator, but because he knew where Lily was, and he still had a boat and a plan.

"You remember," Ras said.

"I'll never forget. How did you learn to sail a ship?" he replied.

"Ain't no ship," Ras chuckled.

"Bigger than those boats back at the beach. How did you learn?"

Ras looked at him. The Boy squinted into the sun.

"When I was 'bout yo' age I would go wit' the Reverend. We would fill the boat up wit' slaves who wanted to come here. Best time of my life."

Ras talked about the weather, the wind, and the waves. He talked about tides and currents and how the moon had something to do with all of it. He admitted with a grin that he did not know the how and why. The Boy and the other two men listened. The horse's ears turned back and forth often as if to listen also. Even the slain alligator lying in the skiff stared up at the back of Ras.

Weeks passed as he worked all day with Ras, milking out the specialized knowledge. He spent some of each night with the boats, carving out the rotted wood and laying in fresh wood. Each night he passed through the baby farm he lingered a little longer, searching the open windows and doors for a glimpse of Lily. The buildings were usually still except for the occasional baby wailing and a few candles burning. More than one night he found white men gathered on the other side of the street. They stood at the barred doors and seemed to watch like the others, the difference being the doors were wide open. He disappeared quickly on these nights.

The work on the boat was almost complete. He had made a choice between the two remaining hulls and poured his efforts into that one. He handmade the wooden tree nails used to fasten new planks to the old. He used stone to grind down the rough edges and make smooth the hull. He managed to hide weeks' worth of the hard biscuits he had for breakfast, along with a heavy bladder full of fresh water. Every day felt electric. He was ready to go.

The horses listened as the Boy explained how the stars lived in groups and if you memorized the groups, you could read the sky like a map. It was his way of trying to remember everything Ras had told him over the last few months.

Talking to the horses had become one of the best parts of his day. The way they looked like they were listening made him laugh. He thought of old Tom often and his bond with the horses. He hoped Tom was doing well but knew deep inside that he wasn't. As he saddled up the last one, he realized he would never see these horses again once he escaped to freedom. He secured the last cinch and apologized. The horse raised his head and showed his teeth in a comical way. The Boy smiled and the horse whinnied, did a little dance, and showed his teeth again.

He thought about how good the horses were treated. Their days were filled with work and decent food. They had a strong, dry shelter to rest in. He questioned why he was trying so hard to leave this place. He had a purpose here. It wasn't his favorite work, but he did it well and he was finally starting to fit in with the others. His heart was jumping in his chest and he wondered what in the world had he been thinking. He'd spent so much energy fixing the boats, so much time plotting his escape.

"Escape what?" he asked the horses. He thought about all the time and encouragement Ras had given him, all the things he had taught him. He looked down at the large hooves and remembered how terrified he had been the first time Ras had shown him how to change the horse's shoes. He remembered falling off the giant beast and Ras laughing and teasing him until he climbed back on. He thought about planting and picking tobacco. He remembered fighting for everything back then. He remembered fighting for his life. It was Ras that had saved him from that life. He could hear the cobbler's words about freedom and they struck him as foolish. Talk of choice and self-determination seemed misguided and irresponsible. Ras cared about him; he took care of him.

The Boy realized that Ras was the only man in his entire life who had ever cared for him. Looking down at his alligator boots he felt like he belonged here after all. He thought back to his bare feet, callused and filthy. He remembered killing the cook's helper, but the noise of the cat and hammer did not come. Maybe he had killed the man for a reason.

Memories came rushing up, his room above the barn, his books, Lily and old Tom, his master, her dead eyes, the shotgun blast, the blood. He felt disgusted with how weak he used to be. His tears tasted like venom. It was Ras, this place, that made him the man he had become. Why would he ever leave?

The Boy settled into his breakfast, thinking about how nice it was that the old cook and his little helper worked so hard. A hot meal twice a day was something for any man to cherish. He finished and watched the other men eat. He watched Ras hold court at the middle of the long table and looked forward to the day. The Boy had learned to frame his work as duty and no longer wished this or wished that about it. He accepted it as something he had been trusted to do, and he did it to the top of his ability. He was learning this about every aspect of his life. Removing how he felt about something made it simply a task to complete or a problem to solve."Don't demand things to happen as you wish, but wish things to happen as they do and you will be well," popped into the Boy's head from nowhere. He knew it came from a book on master Conner's shelf, but he never understood what it meant until this very moment. Grinning ear to ear he scraped his dish and rushed to gather Ras's horse.

"Boy, you look like someone tryna pick yo' cotton," Ras said with a grin from atop his horse. The Boy stared up at Ras with the new boy in the saddle behind him, and their matching grins.

"We gonna show dis little one how it's done today." He turned his horse and cantered toward the fields. The young boy taunted him, straining his neck to keep eye contact as long as he could.

In the field the Boy tried not to watch Ras and the new boy but couldn't help himself. He cursed to himself through gritted teeth. He could hear Ras and the boy laughing. He could feel them stop and watch when he put the cane to work. Because they watched, he drew blood every time. He hoped the young boy was terrified by the violence. But every time he glanced over his shoulder toward Ras, the boy was grinning and staring. It seemed the young boy had violence in him. Just like Ras.

Two more days passed with Ras paying attention to the new cook's helper. The Boy felt something slipping away.

In the early morning twilight, the Boy stood in the line of men waiting for breakfast. He watched the young boy work like he was watching a memory, or a dream of a memory. He could see himself chipping wood with the small hatchet to stoke the fire, cutting chitterlings into the pot, and gathering empty tin plates from the long wooden tables. The cook snapped him out of his reverie with "Hey, boy, gimme yo' plate!" The Boy looked to the cook with his plate pushed forward. He hoped for some sort of affectionate recognition from the old man. He got a plate full of mess and nothing else. As he turned he locked eyes with the new boy and saw a hard malice. He did his best to imitate the cold sneer.

The Boy walked the fields in a trance. He noticed Ras was alone on his horse and went into a state of daydream. He struggled with his feelings of contempt. He was torn betwe-en hate and concern for the young boy. He wondered if Ras cared more for the new boy. He imagined taking the place of Ras and becoming the man in charge. He fantasized about how he would run things with a kinder hand if he were in control. He looked past Ras, up on the ridge a quarter mile out he noticed another man on a horse, with a rifle, and remembered who was in charge. Or more importantly who was not in charge.

That night he lay awake. He decided he would not let Ras force him to hate the innocent boy. He resolved to bond with the new boy, to win him over. He dreamed of clever ways to make the boy see that they were the same, that they could help each other. He was wondering what it would feel like to have a friend when the door moved on its leather hinge.

"You awake?"

The Boy froze. The door pushed in slow, and he recogni-zed the small silhouette of the new boy crouched in his open doorway.

"I need yo' help." Almost too soft to be heard.

"Come on in," the Boy said. He felt the young boy wanted to be friends. He felt an odd warmth as the door closed behind his guest."What you need?" he asked as he rose to his elbows. He smiled and hoped the boy could see it and feel safe. With the door closed the moon light shone through in fragments, one of which glinted off the steel in the young boy's hand.

The first blow glanced off the side of his head with a sting. He managed to grab hold of his attacker's wrist before a second swing. The young boy used his free hand to strike. It landed on the opposite ear, but he was small and not very strong. The scuffle lasted less than a minute. The Boy was too strong for his young opponent. With his knife in his chest and a crushed windpipe it took another quiet minute for him to die. Even in the dark he could see that the knife in the young boy's chest belonged to Ras. Hot tears fell onto the dead boy and he knew he had to escape, tonight.

The Boy gathered his favorite horse and walked the first half mile. He reeled over what had just happened. Despite his jealousy he had never wanted to kill the boy, but why did the boy try to kill him?

"Did Ras put him up to it?" he asked the horse. He loved and hated Ras all at once. He contemplated going back and killing Ras in his sleep. He thought about going back to apologize to Ras, he wondered if Ras would forgive him. He remembered the death in the little boy's eyes and vowed to escape. He focused his energy on finding Lily as he climbed onto the horse's bare back. He fantasized about how happy Lily would be to see him, how proud she would be and how excited she would be when he told her he was taking her to freedom.

She screamed when he found her. She had been sitting in the same rocking chair as the last time he'd laid eyes on her. She was dressed as if waiting for him. When he bent to her and shook her gently, she opened her eyes and gasped at his giant smile. Then she screamed. He froze, his smile froze, his heart froze, but the panic had already rushed in and he hit her hard across the face with an open hand. In her shocked eyes he could see the old barn, the sun coming in through the roof, the dust in the air, and himself throwing a tantrum. He remembered the panic in her and now understood it. He felt sick. He recalled complaining about being hungry and thirsty as she risked everything for him. His face burned with shame as he remembered the shotgun so close to exploding all over them and his own oblivion.

"Lily! It's me," he shouted in a whisper."We gotta go! I'm gonna take us outta here!"

Her blank stare felt louder than the scream, but she remained silent."I got a boat! We gonna leave this place!"

He searched her blank stare for some kind of recognition but found nothing. He stood her up. "Lily, it's me," he repeated, shaking her gently.

"Get out!" she yelled. "Get out!" pointing a shaking finger towards the door.

"Lily, it's me! I'm gonna get us outta here!"

She pulled away hard as he tightened his grip on her. "No!" rang out into the quiet night and forced his resolve. He raised his hand and she covered her head. Her muscles relaxed and surrendered. He still held her as they moved toward the door and surveyed the empty road. He glanced back at Lily; her eyes watched the ground in front of her. She had given up the struggle against this man like so many times before. A lamp lighted in the next window. They moved into the night.

They hit the beach near midnight. The moon was full and the tide was high. He had to wade knee deep into the water to get to the small boat and untie it and bring it back towards the beach. The thought of alligators almost drowned out the adrenaline until he had the skiff's bow in the mud. He kept one eye on the trail and the other on Lily as he searched for his stash of food and water. The water was there but the food bag was empty and riddled with holes.

He had to lift Lily into the boat, he noticed she weighed nothing. Pushing the skiff off the beach proved difficult. His mind reeled with panic as he struggled and pushed, his feet digging into the sandy mud. Lily sat at the bow looking into her lap and he realized she should be near the back of the boat, or stern, as Ras had taught him. He hopped aboard and as calmly as he could he moved her back past the small mast and tattered canvas sail. As soon as he sat her down he could feel the boat lift a little and rock back and forth. His heart leapt as he grabbed an oar and shoved against the beach from inside the boat.

When he felt the boat break free, he sat and locked the oar in its place. With his back to Lily he fumbled for the second oar and found its lock also. He turned the boat around and began pushing forward through the opening in the mangrove trees. The moon illuminated the water like a lighted path, and he rowed for the widest channels. After a while the silence along with the twisting and turning began to overwhelm him. He began to second guess himself, the plan, everything. He started to believe he was lost, rowing in circles through the swampy mangroves.

He was sweating thinking about all the things that could happen to them if they got caught. Looking back at Lily curled up on the bottom of the boat brought him back to his senses. The mangrove branches scraped his head and pulled at his hair. He rowed hard and had the boat going forward again. An hour later the mangroves opened to flat, calm, moonlit water as far as he could see. A sense of accomplishment mixed with dread filled him with energy. He had made it out of the forest of mangrove trees, but the cobbler had warned him that this was only the beginning, that it would get more dangerous from here.

He'd been told that a mile or so from shore the sea would turn into a very different animal. Another hour of rowing and he started to think the cobbler had been wrong about some things; the water was as smooth as glass. Lily slept. He paused to watch her for a moment to make sure she was breathing. She seemed like a hollow shell of herself. He was afraid for her.

The group of stars that Ras had shone him was bold in the sky and he rowed towards them with purpose. Ras explained that he could use the sky like a map. These particular stars would lead a man and his boat west. As they faded into the horizon the sun would be coming up at his back, and if he kept it there he would still be heading west. So that's what he did, even if he was unsure if Ras had been telling the truth.

With dawn creeping up and out behind him he felt a little surer of himself and his teacher. He also noticed a breeze. Up ahead the water looked darker. It didn't have the smooth sheen he'd grown used to during the night. He wondered if this was the danger he'd been warned about by the cobbler. Ras had told him so many things, he found it hard to remember any of it. He thought about the old blind man that knew things he shouldn't and saw things a blind man couldn't. He wondered how he'd died so suddenly when he'd seemed so healthy. Then he realized that maybe the old man had escaped into the night. He smiled at the thought.

The spray on his face shook him from his racing thoughts. He noticed the canvas sail was struggling free of the ropes that bound it. The sound of it fluttered and the boom, as Ras called it, began to jerk to the left and stop hard by another rope. He began to recall his instructions piece by piece. As he looked at the sail, along with a tangle of ropes, he wondered for the first time if the cobbler had been telling the truth all along. Had that old, blind man been around the world, had he seen and done things people only read about in books? It seemed impossible.

The back end of the boat started to swing into the wind. He struggled with the oars, trying to right the boat and put the early sun on his back again. He looked at the sail again and realized that it was time to let it fly. He untied two of the three small ropes that held the sail in a bunch against the mast. As he reached for the third knot the canvas exploded open, knocking the small boat onto its side.

He was in the water as he watched the boat right itself, but the mast lay lazy, half in the water, half in the boat. He panicked and began swimming. The boat began to fall off the wind, coming straight to him as he grabbed at the side and struggled to pull himself up and into the boat. His breath heaved as he surveyed the wrecked mast and rotted canvas spread out over the water. In a tiny corner of his mind he heard violent splashing and felt grateful to be out of the water. He turned and saw Lily drowning. She splashed and choked and flailed an arm's length away. He moved towards the oars, but the boat was a disaster. He looked back at Lily. She was double the distance away. He began cutting through ropes and canvas like a man possessed. He threw canvas overboard and pulled some in. He did anything he could do to separate the boat from the floating wreckage. Cutting and dragging canvas and looking back to a flailing Lily. Cursing and using all his strength he managed to get the mast free of the half-swamped boat. The splashing had stopped. Lily was no longer flailing about. He took a deep breath and steeled himself to look back. He watched her dip under. He felt the boat pivot under him. He moved toward the stern, ready to swim to her, to let the boat go on the journey alone, when she surfaced.

Her face had relaxed and for the first time she looked at him. He watched her float onto her back and spread her arms, her white gown flowing around her like blurry angel wings. She leaned forward and began to swim to the boat, to him. He pulled her aboard fast, expecting her to be heavy like the canvas sail. Falling backwards they lay on the bottom, panting as the boat steadied. The wind had vanished, the morning dead still.

Lily sat in the bow wrapped in what was left of the canvas sail. He rowed thinking about what the Cobbler had told him. "Facing forward as you row will make it easier to stay on course, but you can row with more power facing backward." He had kept the rising sun on his back but now it was directly overhead, and his skin burned. Sweat evaporated too fast to cool his cooking skull. He struggled to keep shade over him with his shirt. The heat pushed down hard into the small boat. The leather pouch of sweet water somehow stayed in the boat, surviving the knock down. He could hear it sloshing behind him. The only other sounds were the oars and their creaking locks.

Lily had not spoken. He hoped she would be joyful, but she had not said a word, so he filled in the silence. He talked about the island. He started at the beginning as if it were a story from a book. He explained how he found his way in the tobacco fields. He left out the crying. He did not mention the beatings, or the theft. He described the surface of it all, as if he had been a visitor. He mentioned Ras as someone who"kind of helped me out a couple times, showed me a few things." He left out the violence and the killing.

The sun dipped low and burned into his face, he changed positions. Letting go of the oars he felt his skin stick to the wooden handles. Blood ran down his hands and forearms. His palms were blistered and torn, the color of raw pork. He turned on the bench seat so that his back faced the sun and the bow of the boat, where Lily sat wrapped in the canvas. He grimaced as he gripped the oars. They felt cold with blood and sweat. He pulled instead of pushed. It felt good to change. He felt good inside that he was so much stronger than he used to be. He rowed.

He started to doubt the cobbler again. His warning that the ocean could be a monster, that it would swallow you whole seemed less and less likely. It had been all night and all day, and back into night again and the sea remained as flat as the cobbler's tanning pit or a slick of pig grease in the yard. He felt relief, he had made it through the hard part. He kept rowing through the molasses.

"I was born free." The sound startled him.

"I was born in France." He felt the words on his back as the sun dipped into the sea. His whole body tingled hearing Lily's voice so close, so real. "There was a war, we had to leave. I had a sister. And a mother." He rowed. "My mama was beautiful. Tall and black. She was born in Kenya. I remember the ship. It was a long hard trip from France. The rats. I wish we had never left." He had never heard her cry. He rowed. She sobbed.

Nautical twilight glowed on the horizon and a deep black followed them toward it. He lifted the working ends of the oars into the boat and sat still. He began shivering as the sweat and toil pushed back against the cool night air.

"Come rest," Lily offered. He wrapped into the canvas with her.

"What happened to your family?" he asked, more to the night than to Lily.

"I found you, boy."

"But what happened to your sister and mother, your father? I don't understand."

"Me neither, boy. I don't understand."

"What happened?" he asked her directly. She began to sob again.

"We were rich. We had everything. We owned slaves. But it must not have been enough."

"Why, what happened?" He sounded like a child as he asked her again.

"He sold us. My mother, my sister and me, he sold us like the rest of them." This time it was the Boy whose eye stung with tears. Lily wrapped an arm around him and they slept. They floated on the dark, flat water and slept.

He ripped the canvas from his face and stared into the blue sky. Soaked with sweat and a little panicked, his mind raced to understand where he was. Seeing Lily bent over the back of the boat brought him closer. Feeling his balloon-like hands and seeing them cracked and bloody brought him back to the here and now. He pulled himself up and sat on the bench. His tongue and throat burned. The sun cooked his sweat dry in seconds, but he was happy to see it behind them as it should be. They were still on course. *On course for where?* he thought to himself.

Not wanting to sound fearful, he tried cheerily to ask Lily what she was doing but the words wouldn't come. He realized he was breathing uneasy and reached for the small cask of sweet water at Lily's feet. She turned at the same time and filled the cask with a cupped handful of sea water. She was startled by him, then smiled. "Drink, boy. You look like you gonna fall over dead." She turned and scooped another handful and drank. "It's salty, but there's plenty of it."

"The salt water will kill you. Do not drink the salt water." The sentence echoed in his head. He had heard it from the cobbler. Ras had said something similar. He didn't know why it was dangerous.

"Stop!" he croaked, not recognizing his own voice. "Stop drinking that!" It felt like his throat was bleeding and on fire at the same time.

"Ain't you thirsty?" Lily begged. "I been at it all morning, but the more I drink the thirstier I get. Don't make no sense."

He took a palm full and put it to his lips. It burned his hands; it burned his lips. It burned everything it touched all the way down.

"You can't drink it," he said as he lifted the cask to the side and poured it overboard.

"I been filling that up. What are you doing?"

"If you drink the sea water you will die." he whispered best he could.

"You ungrateful little motherfucker! You ain't changed a bit! You still just a spoilt little boy! You snatch me from the best work I ever had. You tell me a bunch of lies about you dis and you dat! You think you savin' us, you killed us! We already dead, boy!"

She was screaming, wild. Spitting and sobbing as she hurled the words out through cracked, inflamed lips. He was confused and terrified, but he knew she was right. They had no food, no water, no idea where they were going. He scanned the horizon and saw only heat rippling up off the dead flat ocean. It reminded him of a story about a man lost in the desert, cooking under a heavy sun with nothing but sand to drink. Everything was so still and solid looking that he wondered if he could get out of the boat and start walking.

Lily tucked herself into the tiny shade at the back of the boat. The outburst had taken its toll. She curled up in a tiny ball and slept. He put the oars into the water and began to row.

His tears burned his burnt face. The salt on his tongue enraged him. He wanted to scream but he knew he couldn't. He turned to face the front of the boat and continued to row.

"I'm sorry, Lily." he said, mostly to himself but loud enough to hear if she were listening. "I'm sorry for everything. I don't know why I remembered master Conner teaching me to read and write. I know she didn't do none of that. I know it was you. It was you that did all of it. You was the only one that ever did anything for me, and I treated you bad and treated her like she was my mama or somethin'. I don't know why I did that but I'm sorry." He cried to himself but no more tears came.

"Your mama was my friend. She was beautiful and my only friend," Lily whispered. "Your daddy was a weak man, a coward, but I think he loved your mama. Or maybe he was just weak."

"What happened to her?" he asked.

"Master Conner was a hateful person. Just like her daddy, she was mean. She sold your mama the day you was weaned. I think she did it mostly to hurt your daddy. To teach him some kinda lesson."

He rowed and wondered, trying to understand what Lily was saying. "I don't understand," he said finally.

"Me neither, baby," she replied.

The two minutes felt like days until she spoke again. "Ian. Ian was your daddy. And he shot himself. Just like his daddy. His daddy shot himself in front of her, with the same gun. Maybe that was why she was so hateful."

He rowed, trying to put the pieces together but not knowing where or how to start. He rowed until the sun moved to the front of the boat, then he turned himself around and rowed some more. He rowed until a curved, thin line of red separated the two black halves of the world. Then he stowed the oars and they slept under the canvas sail.

When he awoke it was daybreak. The soft light was beautiful. It started at the back of the boat and gradually turned to black just above him. He marveled that the boat was still pointed in the right direction. The beauty disappeared as he thought *There is no direction.*

It took a few moments for him to realize that he was alone in the boat. He got up fast and almost fell forward from the dizziness. He expected to see Lily walking around outside the boat, picking flowers or bringing back something to eat or drink. But he only saw the sky, and a perfect reflection of the sky. He looked over the side of the boat and stared back at himself.

He did not row. He did not move until the sun was high. He covered himself with the canvas, but ripped it away at every tiny sound, expecting Lily to be there. When the sun sank into the sea he uncovered himself and stared at the back of the boat, the last place he had seen her.

A crushing weight kept him captive in the bow of the boat. He covered himself and slept during the day and sat staring at the back of the boat all night. He was sure Lily was still there, he just couldn't see her. The blisters on his hands became deep open sores. His lips swelled and cracked open but did not bleed. His eyes were also swollen and caked shut with mucus. He could only bear to force them open during the cool of the night. After a while he stopped bothering to do even that. He stayed wrapped in the canvas sail day and night, crying without tears. He could hear the cobbler's words about freedom and they cut him like a thousand tiny knives. Talk of freedom stung, he only wanted to be alive.

He knew he was dying of thirst.

When she did come back to him she was not happy. He heard her coming from a ways off, stomping through the water with heavy feet. The only wave in this flat sea she washed over the side and into the boat. She stood upright in the back of the boat and kicked at his sleeping feet. When he finally came out from under the canvas it took all his strength. He struggled to make out her shape, but her voice was piercing and unmistakable.

"Perhaps it has been foolish of me to carry this heavy burden for so long. It was given to me when I was younger than you. I refused to put it down, because putting it down felt like giving up. I held it tighter the day I met you. I tried to share it with you. I hoped you would see through the folly of this existence. I hoped that you would make your life what you wanted it to be." She shifted the massive book in her arms and chuckled to herself. "Seems like you're trying at least. I'm not sure if you're trying to live or trying to die, but either way the choice is yours. And that's somethin.'"

She raised the book high above her head and threw it down hard onto the Boy.

He didn't quite wake up when his skiff hit the side of the brig, but he heard voices coming from above. He thought *they must be angels.*

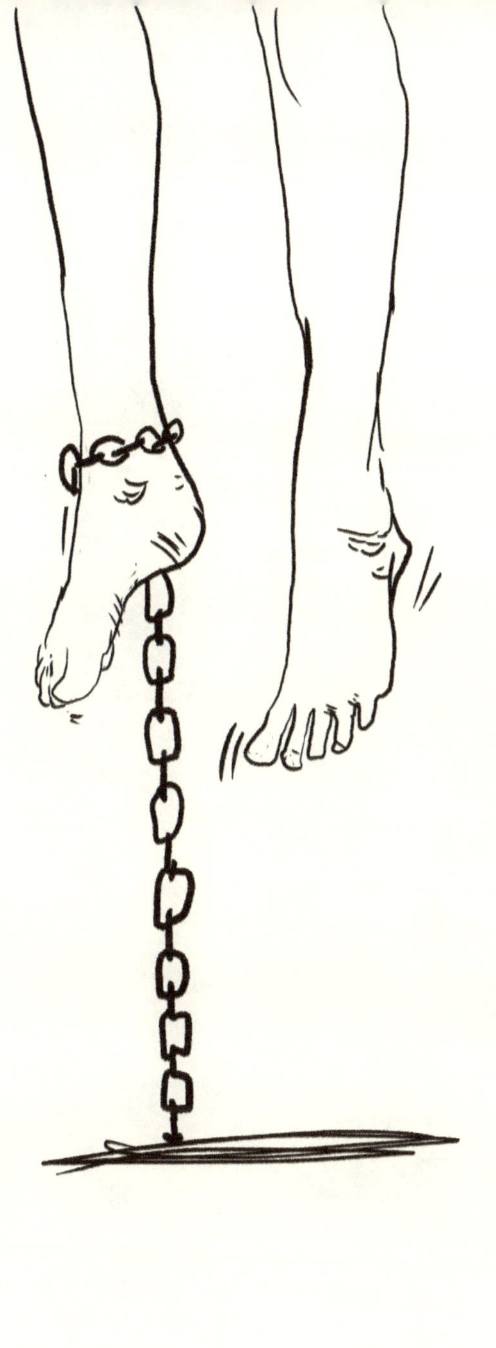